Like my page on Facebook:

https://www.facebook.com/AuthorMisha/

Join my reading group where discussions will be held after each book and sneak peeks are given before the release. There are also visuals of each character.

Yamisha's Bookworm Boulevard

Sometimes I Trip On How Happy We Could Be

Have you ever loved a man so much that it hurt your soul? I mean, like really hurt.

There's no pain like being in love with a man that you must question if he's in love with you.

Things can be so good in the beginning and then you have to question yourself.

You start to continuously question him, and every move that he makes becomes suspect.

Do I really love him? Does he really love me?

Is the woman that is screw facing us just a friend of the family?

Sometimes no matter how much you try, you just aren't meant to be together.

Read my story, rock with me.

There's not always a happy ending.

Prologue

"Aargh,"I screamed as another contraction rippled through my body. Doubling over in pain, I held onto my stomach until the pain passed. Yes, I had been pregnant for 10 months and was ready to get this baby out of me. Yes, it was obvious that the pain would be crucial, but this was a pain that I couldn't imagine. I couldn't make this shit up.

As soon as the pain passed, I was asking everyone in the room the question that I had been asking them for the past 4 hours.

"Where is Storm? Has anybody talked to him?" My mother and Chiasia, looked at each other but said nothing. That gave me my answer right there. I stopped walking around the room, trying to dilate more and walked over to my bed and grabbed my phone.

Dialing Storm's number, it didn't even ring just went straight to voicemail. Throwing the phone on the bed, I yelled as another contraction came. My mother tried to grab my hand, but I waved her off because I didn't want to be touched. The only touch that could put me on ease right now was my man.

The man that had impregnated me was not here in this room. He was somewhere doing god knows what, with god knows who. I swear if this man came in here and he hadn't lost a limb, we were going to have a fucking issue.

Closing my eyes, I sat on the edge of the hospital bed and took a deep breath. This shit wasn't real, it couldn't be. He wasn't going to miss the birth of our baby, my first born. Nah, he wasn't going to do that to me.

"Chiasia, call Chinx, do whatever you have to do, but get Storm here and get him here NOW!"

Just as she went out into the hallway to make the calls, the nurse was coming in to check my cervix again. Quite frankly, I was tired of this hoe coming in here putting her finger in my vagina, but I didn't really have a choice.

"Ok, honey. I need you to lay on your back, so I can check and see how dilated you are." Without a word, I laid on my back and waited to feel her latex covered fingers, invade my space. She did it quicker than before, probably because she could sense the aggravation emitting from my body. It was all over my face.

"You are about 7 centimeters. We're almost there." She went over to the computer that was in the corner of the room, and started typing information in. Despite me not responding to her she still had a smile on her face. She was probably used to dealing with hormonal women in labor.

Deciding to lay on my back for a moment, I closed my eyes and did the breathing exercises that we had practiced in the birthing classes. I didn't really think that class was useful, but as the next contraction came, it didn't feel as bad as I tried to breathe through it.

"Do you want any ice or anything?" my mother asked. She was trying to be helpful, but for some reason her voice was irritating me every time she spoke. Maybe because Storm's voice was the one that I really wanted to hear.

"Yes, can you get me a cup of ice please?" She nodded her head up and down then headed out the door. The nurse asked if there was anything I needed and when I declined she followed suit. Now, I finally had a peace of mind, but again here I was alone; without the father of my child.

I heard the door open, and I figured it was my mother or Chiasia coming back into the room, but then I smelled his cologne. It was mixed with some other scents and I knew I was going to cause hell in this room.

Opening my eyes, I laid my eyes on Storm Castro. His eyes were bloodshot red, and I could tell he was high, or drunk, maybe both. His hair that had grown so much since I met him, was pulled up into a messy bun. His eyes met mine and he knew he had fucked up.

"Where the fuck were you? Aarghhh," another contraction came before I could even get his response. He rushed to my side and tried to grab my hand, but I pulled away. When the contraction went away, I went off.

"You black ass, no good ass nigga. You're already late as fuck getting here and you have the nerve to come in here smelling like weed, liquor, and sex." When he got closer to me the smell of sex was all over him. "You didn't even have the decency to take a shower?" I raised my hand to slap him, but he stopped it mid strike.

"Ya black ass better chill the fuck out girl. I wasn't out fucking nobody, I fell asleep at Chinx's house." The lie rolled right off his tongue. Surprisingly, I laughed, this was the funniest shit ever. Here I was, praying that he was ok. Deep down inside, I knew he wouldn't miss his baby girl's arrival for anything dumb.

I was half expecting to hear he had been shot or found in a ditch somewhere. That maybe his dope dealer ways had caught up to him. But nope, his ass had actually been out cheating on me while I was in pain birthing his child.

"What's so funny?" he asked with a perplexed look on his face.

"This." Pushing the button for the nurse, it took just under 1 minute for her to appear in my room.

"Yes?" she asked. It was the same nurse that had checked my cervix.

"Can you get security to escort him out of my room please?"

"Are you sure?" she asked with a confused look on her face.

"Yes, I'm 100% sure. We've been getting along fine today, let's not start. Just get him the hell out of my room." She looked from Storm to me and closed the door.

Now I had pissed him off, but who cares? He was being disrespectful as fuck.

"Get the fuck out of here. You gonna have them crackers come and make me get out ya room? You done fell and bumped ya fucking head Skyy."

I closed my eyes and tuned him out; this pain was way more important. My daughter coming into this world healthy was way more important. He was supposed to help with that, but he was sitting here stressing me out in the little time he had actually been in the room. Nah, he could get out, I didn't even care anymore.

The door opened and Chiasia and my mother entered the room. Right behind them was security and I pointed to Storm, directing them to the trash.

"What's going on? What's wrong?" my mother asked.

"He needs to go." That was all the explanation I was willing to give.

"So, you're not going to let me see the birth of my daughter? Are you fucking serious Skyy?"

I played mum. I didn't say a word and if a person didn't know I could hear, then they would honestly think I was deaf.

"Iight," he responded nodding his head up and down. "I'm out, I don't need to be put out. But you remember this shit."

2 excruciating hours later and my daughter entered this world. She was the spitting image of me, and her chocolate skin was

pretty and smooth. Even her cries sounded pretty as the nurses worked fast to clean her off and measure her length and weight.

Once they were done they laid her on my chest, and she calmed down immediately. It was like she knew who I was. All those months of talking to her while in my womb had paid off. My baby knew her mother.

"What are you naming her?" the nurse asked.

"Sun," I responded. "Sun Jones." I could see the shock in my peripheral on my mom and Chi's face because I wasn't giving her Storm's last name. He didn't deserve it, he couldn't even make an appearance for her arrival.

"That's it? No middle name?"

"Nope, she doesn't need it. People will be too intrigued by her first name anyway."

Chapter 1

Skyy

Knock, knock "Wake up Skyy, it's time for school!" my mother yelled through my closed door. *Knock, knock*

She would keep knocking until I answered, so taking my head from under the comforter I responded," Okay, I'm getting up ma."

Turning over, I looked at the clock and it was 6:30. I had to be at school by 7 which was a 10-minute walk; so, I had 20 minutes to get myself together.

Hopping out of the bed I walked down the hallway to brush my teeth and do my hair. Showering the night before was a daily routine for me since I knew I would be in a mad dash in the morning. Rushing back to my room, I grabbed my outfit for the day that was already on a hanger in the closet. My outfit was something basic, I never liked to stand out too much and I didn't have the money to anyway.

It was a nice hot day, so I was wearing a pair of shorts that were tight fitted and stopped just above my knee, a cream-colored V-neck shirt and a pair of sandals were on my feet. Nothing fancy, but I was comfortable and cute. Grabbing my book bag, I glanced at the clock and I was right on time.

Leaving my room, I looked at my mother's door. It was closed so I didn't even bother saying bye because that only meant one thing; a man was in the room with her. My stomach turned at the thoughts of what was going on in there, but I just shook my head and headed to school.

"Hey Skyy!" my friend Chiasia yelled from the corner. She was always waiting for me at the corner, so we could walk to school together as we did every day.

Waiting until I was closer I replied," Why do you always have to be so loud girl?" I asked her in a hushed tone.

"Girl, cause that's just how I am loud, proud and so fucking fine."

I shook my head as we started the walk towards school. Chiasia was loud and obnoxious, but she was my best friend; my only friend. Even though she was loud and was always the loudest one wherever we were, she had a good heart and a great personality. Chiasia was also pretty, as she always reminded everyone.

She was light skinned and had long hair that was a sandy brown, but she always dyed it black or covered it with a sew in. She also had a nice body that all the boys stared at because it was a body that made her look like she was well over the 17 years that she was. I, on the other hand was the complete opposite. Yes, I was pretty but my skin tone, was a deep dark chocolate; my hair was shoulder length, and it was as dark as my skin. Just like Chiasia my body was on point, and the boys loved to stare. I had ample breasts, a plump ass and a flat stomach to match.

"You a damn mess. Come on so we can get to school, I have a test in first period, and you know I can't be late for Mr. Fitzgerald." Just thinking about being late made me put a little more pep in my step. Maybe a little too much because I didn't even pay attention as I damn near walked into traffic.

Beep

The car and I both came to a halt before I stepped foot into the street.

I'm taking out this time
To give you a piece of my mind

(Cause you can't knock the hustle)

Who do you think you are?

Baby one day you'll be a star

Last seen out of state where I drop my sling

I'm deep in the South kicking up top game

Bouncing on the highway switching four lanes

Screaming through the sunroof, money ain't a thang

Your worst fear confirmed

Me and my fam roll tight like The Firm

Getting down for life, that's right, you better learn

While I play with fire, you burn

We get together like a choir, to acquire what we desire

The car creeped up once it noticed I was stopped and rolled the window down. To say my breath was caught in my throat was an understatement. I had lost my ability to talk. This man behind the wheel was so handsome.

"Yo, you good?" Instead of answering, I just nodded my head up and down. "Make sure you watch where you walking, ma. You're too beautiful to get hit by a car."

Still not answering, I nodded again. The man behind the wheel just chuckled as he pulled off.

"Girl, you standing here like a damn deer caught in headlights. Why wouldn't you say anything to Storm?"

"Storm? Who's he?"

Chiasia looked at me as if I had just said I didn't recognize a legend. "You don't know who Storm is?" she asked like she was appalled. Not even giving me time to respond, she told me all about Storm as we continued on our way to school. By the time, we walked into school she had given me the whole run down on Storm.

He was sexy as hell, but from what she was telling me, the chocolate man and I had nothing in common. Chiasia let me know that he was a known drug dealer from around the way. All the niggas feared him, and the bitches wanted to be with him. She was surprised that I hadn't ever heard of him, but I didn't know why.

Besides school, I didn't go anywhere else. I was what you would refer to as a square. I stayed out of the way and minded my business; she knew this. After she ran down all this man's business, I asked her the golden question.

"How do you know all of this?"

"You know my cousin Quiana and how she be knowing everything. Oh yea, she's having a party this weekend and we're going!" she practically yelled while we walked down the hall. If it wasn't for everyone else being loud, we would have been the center of attention right now.

"You know I'm not going to any party, especially at Quiana's house," I looked at her like she was going crazy. Quiana lived in one of the most ghetto parts of Rochester. They called it The Bricks; my ass had never been, and I didn't plan on going. Thankfully, it was on the other side of the town from where I lived, so I never had to pass by it or anything.

"Oh, my gosh Skyy, stop being so damn wack. Live a little, we're seniors and we deserve it. We'll be graduating this weekend, just think of it as a graduation party for us," she said as she brushed her shoulder against me as she started doing a little shake with her shoulders.

"Yea, I don't know. I'll let you know," I replied as I turned to head into my 1st period class.

"We're going!" Chiasia yelled as I walked into my class, shaking my head. Yea, she thought I was going but that night I would be home playing sick.

"Look at my baby," my mom squealed covering her mouth with both hands. It was the day of my graduation. The day I was setting out to be an adult in the real world. My mother and I had gone to the mall, shopping for hours to find the perfect outfit for this day. We had found a red, flowing dress that hugged my curves in all the right places.

At first, I was real hesitant about the dress, but my mom insisted; honestly, I thought that it hugged my curves just a little too much. But right now, looking at my reflection I was very pleased with her decision. The dress made me look older than I was, I looked like I was ready to venture out in the world.

"You look beautiful Skyy." My mother had tears in her eyes. "Wait a minute, I have something else for you." Rolling my eyes as she walked out of the room, I sat on the edge of my bed.

She was making a really big deal out of this, but it was only a graduation ceremony. That's just how my mom was though. She made a big thing out of everything. Opening the shoe box that was on the floor, I took out a pair of brand new, black Chanel wedge sandals.

They weren't too high, but they were high enough, and I was hoping I could make it through the whole ceremony with these shoes on. Just as I finished strapping my feet into the shoes my mom walked back into the room with a jewelry box in her hand. Immediately, I noticed the jewelry box; it was the one that my grandmother had given to her before she died.

As a little girl, I always loved the jewelry box, I would stare at it and want to touch it, but my mother would never allow me to. At first, I didn't understand, but the older I became, the more I understood the sentimental value of the box and what was held within. Opening the box, my mother took out a pair of diamond earrings and a diamond tennis bracelet.

"I've been waiting for this special day to give this to you. This is your graduation present from your grandmother. She always told me to give it to you when you accomplished something great and graduating at the top of your class is something great." My mother was a bag of water as she put the necklace on me.

"Thank you mom." She turned me around and gave me a hug. I could feel the tears falling on my shoulder. "Mom, come on. We have to go before I'm late."

"Don't try to get out of this loving," she said as she got one last squeeze before letting me go.

Chapter 2

Skyy

"Chiasia, I have nothing to wear, I'm not going." She had been trying to talk me into going to this party for the longest. We were at her house, and she had told me we were just going to chill and watch movies, but now she was trying to drag me to her cousin's party, and I wasn't with it.

"Skyy, stop being so damn boring. We graduated today bih! We should be at the party, having fun, maybe a couple of shots, smoke a blunt or two."

Giving her the side eye, she bust out into laughter. Being the homebody that I was, I had never smoked or drank.

"I'm just playing, but we are going. So, come on get up!" I was sitting on the edge of her bed, and she grabbed my arm, pulling me up and to her closet. "You can just wear something I haven't wore yet."

Going into her closet, I began to look at the clothes on the hangers. The only reason I was looking was to make her feel better because I wasn't going. After 5 minutes of fake browsing, I turned around, but she was standing there with her arms folded, looking at me with a 'yea, right' look on her face.

"You play too much. Let me find you something." Chiasia, went past me and went in her closet. It wasn't even a minute later until she was turning around with something for me to wear. It was a pair of black, distressed high waist shorts and a raspberry colored, tank top bodysuit. I could admit, it was cute, but it wasn't something that I would normally wear.

"I'm not wearing that."

"Why not? You always want to be covered up, it's okay to show some of those curves you got girl. Niggas might look, but I swear they won't bite. Well, Terry used to bite my ass but that's another story," she said with a laugh.

"No, but seriously Skyy, put this on with your wedges, and I'll put some light makeup on you. Yesssss, and I'll be wearing this lil red number tonight." She held up a red, spaghetti strap bodycon dress.

Everything in my head was telling me not to go, but what would one night hurt? I never did anything, went anywhere and I deserved to enjoy summer before I started college in September. Before I knew it, I was agreeing to go to the party, and I was hoping it was something that I didn't regret.

As soon as we got to The Bricks, I felt a nervous feeling in the pit of my stomach. There were niggas littered all around the parking lot. There was no way for us to get to Quiana's house without having to go through them, and I hated that awkward moment. The moment you know that they're watching you from behind, specifically your ass.

Chiasia leaded the way; she was looking cute in her dress with a pair of black heels on and a black clutch purse. Her face was beat to the gawds, and I had to admit, the outfit she picked out for me was cute too. The only thing I didn't like was my ass was threatening to spill out of the shorts and I had to keep pulling them down to make sure my ass was covered.

As we walked through a group of dudes, I made sure to pull down my shorts right before. I was not trying to give anybody out here a sneak peek of my ass. We walked through and just like I thought, they stared us the fuck down.

One dude looked familiar though, it was the one that had almost hit me with his car.

Before I knew what was happening, my heart started to pick up speed; it felt like it was beating out of my chest. We locked eyes before I turned away and continued to Quiana's house. We got to her door and as soon as we opened it, the smoke and smell of weed hit us in the face.

The apartment was packed, and people were standing wall to wall. The music was loud, and the bass had the apartment jumping.

Count 100, 000 in your face (in your face)

Yeah, they put 300 right in the safe

Met her today, oh

She talk to me like she knew me, yeah

Go to sleep in a Jacuzzi, yeah

Yeah, wakin' up right to a two piece, yeah

Countin' that paper like loose leaf, yeah

Gettin' that chicken with blue cheese, yeah

Yeah, boy you so fat like my collar

You snakin', I swear to God that be that Gucci, ay

And you know we winnin' (winnin')

Yeah, we is not losin'

Try to play your song, it ain't move me (what?)

Saw your girl once now she choose me, yeah

We squeezed through the crowded room and headed to the kitchen. Chiasia said that she would probably still be in there making jungle juice and some food to eat. As we got closer to the kitchen, I knew she was in there because I could her loud voice over the music that was playing. The kitchen wasn't nearly as packed as the rest of the house.

"Heyyyy, lil cousin," Quiana squealed. Chiasia was her favorite little cousin and she always showed her hella love when she saw her. "My bad, I couldn't come to see you walk that stage, but momma wasn't watching lil Ray Ray while I came to that and while I shook my ass all night.

Quiana was your typical hood rat. She was nice and all, cool, but her ass was a hood rat. The projects were all she knew and sadly probably all she would ever know. Quiana was nearing her 30's but acted like she had just hit 21. She was cool with all the niggas around the way and at any time you could catch them in her house.

Besides the area she lived in, that was another reason I never accompanied Chiasia when she came over. There were always niggas in and out of her house and that just wasn't my style.

"Girl, it's fine, since this is basically my graduation party and all. I guess I can forgive you," Chiasia responded as she spun around and pointed towards the crowd. In her mind, this was really her party, and she was ready to be the center of attention for the night.

I shook my head and laughed.

"And congrats to you too Skyy. I haven't seen you in forever. You too good for The Bricks?"

"Hell yea, her ass was scared to come tonight," Chiasia responded to her with a laugh.

"No, I was not!" I came to my defense immediately with a laugh. She stayed trying to call somebody out. That was another difference between us. I was so laid back and low key and she was always loud and hype. She loved when all eyes were on her and I'd rather blend into the shadows.

"I'm just playing friend."

"Mmhmm," I responded with a light eye roll.

"What are you making?"

"I'm making some fried chicken and buffalo wing dip. And I'm almost done, these fools won't have me cooking my whole party. Well, your whole party," Quiana joked.

I was on my 2nd cup of jungle juice when Mystikals 'Shake It Fast' came on. No matter how old this song was, it was still an ass shaking classic. The liquor was taking over my body and before I knew it I was in the middle of the floor, dancing with my best friend. The crowd had us hype as I bent over and twerked my ass like a stripper dancing for cash.

Just that quickly, I didn't even care about the too short shorts that I was wearing. The lower cup of my ass was out, and I didn't give a damn. Chiasia was right, this was our time. I had graduated top of my class, and I deserved to have a little fun; I had earned it.

After dancing 3 songs straight, my ass was tired and decided to take a break. Chiasia was following behind me because she was also hot as hell. We decided to go to the bathroom to check on our makeup and I had to pee like crazy.

As soon as we got in the bathroom, with the door closed, Chi started to go in," Girlllll, I didn't know you could dance like that. You've been my best friend all these damn years and been hiding secrets."

Giggling as I pulled the shorts down to use the bathroom, I responded," I didn't even know I could dance like that. This is my first party, I usually just dance in the mirror at home." Once I sat on the toilet to pee, my head started to feel more dizzy, and I realized that I wasn't tipsy anymore; now I was drunk.

"Damn Skyy, you fucked up," Chi said as she touched up her makeup in the mirror.

"Shut up girl, I'm good." After wiping myself, I got up and stood next to her at the sink, so I could wash my hands.

"I got something to mellow us out though." Reaching into her purse, she pulled out an already rolled blunt.

"Where did you get that from?" I asked louder than I needed to.

"If the music wasn't on, everybody would be able to hear your loud, drunk ass."

"My bad, but for real. Where did you get that from?"

"Wellll, you know Chris from our 6th period class?" Nodding my head up and down, I confirmed that I knew who she was talking about. "Yea, so Chris and I have been talking and chilling andddd, long story short I got it from him."

"Why you didn't tell me you talked to him?"

"I don't know," she said with a shrug, but it had to be more than that. Chiasia always told me everything so there had to be a reason she didn't tell me about her and Chris.

"Mmhmm," I responded.

Chiasia lit the blunt and put it to her lips and started to inhale. The strong smell of weed consumed the bathroom.

By the time we left the bathroom I was high as hell. I wasn't a smoker, so by the second time I hit the blunt, I was high. It was my graduation night though and I was ready to get turned up. I was always the good girl, the quiet one who just went to school and got good grades. This was my night to have fun and let loose a bit.

We got back to the living room, and it looked to be a little more crowded. The dance floor seemed a little more packed and as we cut through the crowd I felt a pair of eyes fixated on me, following me. We were in a room full of niggas and I knew niggas liked to stare and watch females walk, but this was different; I could feel the intensity.

Turning my head towards the heat, my eyes met his. If the lights weren't on in this room I wouldn't be able to see him. His skin was dark, as dark as mine and his eyes were dark as well. He was staring right back at me, not even turning his head, he just matched my stare. Storm, it was a good name for him; he looked like he could come fuck some shit up and get me in all types of trouble.

The liquor and weed had me bold, bolder than I would ever be. Biting my bottom lip, I smiled at him and gave him a light wave. He gave me a head nod as he leaned against the wall. Putting the Remy bottle to his lips, he took a sip, and I turned my head and went into the direction Chiasia had gone.

I was so into this man's face that I hadn't even noticed that Chiasia was now across the room. All that time, I had been stuck in place captivated by that man.

"Bitch, how you keep walking and leave me?" I asked her once I reached up to her.

She looked at me with low, red, eyes and laughed," You was all up in Storm's face, so I just wanted to let you have that moment."

"Oh, you feeling that nigga Storm?" Her cousin's friend came out the cut asking. Her name was Amiyah, and I never really liked her ass. She was pretty and all, but there was some shady shit about her, I just couldn't put my finger on. You know how you get that slimy vibe from someone and no matter how much you tried to put it to the side, you just couldn't?

"Nah, not at all. Why, what's up?"

"Oh, nothing. I was just going to tell you that it was a good choice. He sure knows how to work the dick that he has and he is working with a monsta," she said while she took a drink from the red cup she was sipping from.

"Oh," was all I said as I turned my attention back to my friend. Amiyah wanted to make it known that she fucked him and that was some shit I wasn't concerned about. Even if I wanted to fuck with him, that was none of her business because her and I weren't friends.

Realizing I wasn't about to give her any info and the conversation was over, she turned around and headed back to her group of friends. Looking at Chiasia, I gave her the look, and she busted out laughing.

"Bitchhhhh, I can't stand her hating ass either." She knew what I was thinking without me even saying anything. "Who told her ass that we even needed her input?"

"Hahahaha." Chiasia was goofier than usual and laughing like crazy. Just looking at her ass had me laughing as well. I didn't know if the weed was good, or if I was just a lightweight. We talked for a bit and decided we were way too tipsy to be trying to go back to Chi's house tonight, so we decided to stay at Quiana's for the night.

Since we were staying the night, I decided to have another cup of the very potent jungle juice. There was another bowl made and this one was stronger than the last. Deciding I was already too tipsy, I decided to just sip this cup for the rest of the night.

2 hours later and the party was finally dying down. Personally, the weed had worn off and now I was just tipsy and sleepy as hell. Everyone was leaving out, and I watched the door silently hoping that I would see Storm. I had no such luck though, he must have slipped out of here earlier.

I wasn't even going to say anything to him, just needed a glimpse of him. He was cute as hell and all I wanted was another peek of some really good eye candy. Disappointment must have been evident in my face because Chi came and sat next to me on the sofa, asking what was wrong.

"What's wrong with you? Looking like you lost your best friend but I'm right here," she laughed as she nudged me with her shoulder.

"Oh, nothing. I'm just tired."

"Mmhm," she said it as if she didn't believe me. We were best friends, and she knew me like the back of her hand, so she probably knew just who I was looking for and why I was looking so disappointed.

Chapter 2

Skyy

It had been 2 weeks since I graduated, and a week ago I had landed a job at Carl's Burger Shack. It was one of the most popular burger places in our city, so it was always packed. Chi had landed a job here too though, so it wasn't that bad. She was definitely loving the attention of the dudes that came in and out of the place.

Right now, she was supposed to be giving the man at the counter his change, yet she was putting her number in his phone. Shaking my head at her, I couldn't do anything but laugh. He was a cutie though, but he looked a little older.

What am I saying? This man was dressed in a construction uniform, he was undeniably older.

"Skyy, I need you to work the drive thru!" my manager yelled from the back. Rolling my eyes up into my head, I didn't even respond as I headed to the drive thru. A down side of working at this job was having to deal with my incompetent boss; if you could even call him that. Tony was in his late thirties and all he did was sit in the back room and yell out orders.

He yelled out what he wanted us to do and what he wanted the cooks to make for him. Gluttony was a sin, but he didn't seem to know or care about that. Everyday all I thought was that I should contact the producers of My 600 lb life and get him put on the show. Yes, he was that big.

"Welcome to Carl's Burger Shack, what can I get you today?" I asked but there was nothing but silence. In the camera that showed the drive thru, I could see there was an all-black SUV parked there but the windows were still up.

Just a moment later, the windows were rolled down and a voice was coming over the intercom.

"Yo," was all he said like he was waiting for me instead of the complete opposite.

"Welcome to Carl's Burger Shack, what can I get you today?"

"Yea, let me get a number 9 with cheese, no tomatoes or pickles."

"Okay, and what size?"

Cough, cough. "Large."

"What would you like to drink?"

"Uhhh, a Hi-C"

"Fruit punch or orange?"

"Fruit punch."

"Anything else?"

"Nah, that's it."

"Your total is $8.50, come around to the window." The person in the car didn't reply, just pulled up to the first window. Turning around, I placed the cup under the fountain and filled it with light ice and fruit punch. I hated when people filled my cup with all that ice, so I never did it to anyone else.

Covering the cup with a lid, I turned back around and opened the drive thru window. The SUV windows were up again, so all I could see was pitch black tinted windows. The window rolled down slowly, and I swear if he wasn't eye to eye with me, I would be jumping for joy. Like the show Lizzie Mcguire, there was a little cartoon version of me in my head. She was dancing and twerking all over right about now.

Hiding my excitement, I reached out to take the 10-dollar bill he placed in my hand and handed him his drink. Closing the drive thru window back, I finally let out a breath as I got his change. His food was ready, so I checked the bag and prepared to face him again. Avoiding eye contact but not too much, I handed him his change along with his food.

"Have a great day, come back soon." Giving him the routine farewell, but this time I actually meant it. Shit, I should have taken his fries out of the bag, so he would have to turn around.

"Well, I don't know about coming back here, but would I be able to take you out tonight, Skyy?" He had to have gotten my name from the name tag that was pinned to my shirt. "I was going to ask you for ya number a couple of weeks ago at the party, but a nigga had to make moves." Just as I was about to answer him a voice came from behind me.

"Yep, she'll go. What time?" It was Chi being her usual self.

Chuckling, Mr. Handsome himself responded," She can answer for herself shorty. Her pretty ass looked like she was about to say yes anyway."

Blushing, I answered his question as I was about to before," Yes, I will go on a date with you. What time should I be ready?"

"Here," he reached through the window and handed me a rose gold Iphone 6 plus that put my Iphone 4s to shame. "I'll be texting you all the details, iight? See you later beautiful." Just like that, he was off. I could hear the music blasting as he peeled out of the parking lot, and I could just imagine me riding shotgun with him.

"Girllllll," Chi was still standing there, with this big ass grin on her face. For the rest of our shift, all she did was talk about what I should wear, and how I should do my hair and makeup. Since the party, I was now more into makeup and had gotten pretty good with it from watching countless YouTube videos.

It was 7:00 and I had just stepped out of the shower for my date. This was my first one and I was excited as hell, contrary to how nonchalant I acted about it earlier. Storm texted me around 4 letting me know to be ready at 8:30. I had no idea where we were going, but once I told my mother that I was going on a date, she made sure to help me find something to wear.

If it was up to me, I would have been going in a simple outfit on like a pair of jeans and a shirt, but my mother was not letting that happen. Our physique was about the same, so she rummaged through her closet before she found me the perfect dress. It was a rose red, tight fitted dress that stopped right above the knee and it hugged each and every one of my curves.

I had to admit that my mom had picked out a great outfit. The dress was being paired with a pair of nude, strappy sandals and a nude clutch that matched perfectly with it. Most likely we were going to dinner, so the outfit was very appropriate. Hopefully, we weren't doing any kind of activities that I couldn't or shouldn't wear a dress in.

Sitting at my dresser in the furry seat I had made myself with a dusty, old computer chair and some fur, I started to apply my makeup. Since I was still a beginner, I was also watching a makeup YouTube video. It helped me to do mine if I was able to hear that in the background. Today, for this date I wanted to try a smoky eye.

That's why I started my makeup so early; to make sure I had enough time to do this and just in case I fucked it up I had time to do it over. After an hour, my face was beat, smoky eye was popping, and glow was on fleek. I had outdone myself tonight and I couldn't wait to see myself once the dress was on. It was only 30 minutes until Storm was supposed to be here, so I put my hair up into a high bun and got dressed quickly.

At exactly 8:25, I received a text from Storm letting me know that he was outside. My mother was on one of her dates, so she made me promise to send her a picture before I left. In my full-length mirror, I snapped a photo and sent it to her then headed out the door. My nerves were getting the best of me and the butterflies in my stomach were at full force.

Before opening the door, I closed my eyes and took a deep breath. I opened the door, and I swear my heart skipped a beat. There was that fine ass specimen of a man, looking just as cool and collected as ever. He was outside of his truck standing at the passenger door, back leaning against it on his phone.

Once he realized I was out the door, he put his phone in his pocket and I waved hi before turning my back to him, so I could lock the door. I could feel his eyes watching me and taking in everything. If my nerves weren't already getting to me, then they damn sure would have been now. Storm was looking good as hell for our date.

Storm was wearing a pair of black jeans that fitted his physique just right, a red and black Nautica shirt with a Nautica dad hat. On his feet were a pair of black and red Jordans. His wrist was shining with the iced-out watch that he was wearing. He also had a single chain around his neck that was glistening as well. I started towards the car, and he opened the passenger side door.

"Thank you."

"Of course," he responded with a smile, and his shiny white teeth got me excited down below. A feeling I wasn't all that familiar with. No boy or man had ever made me feel this way. Once I slid onto the black, leather seat, Storm closed the door and proceeded to the driver's seat.

"You like surprises?" he immediately asked.

"Ummm, sure why?"

"Just asking. If you play your cards right tonight, get ready for surprises more often," he pulled into traffic, and we started towards our destination.

"Oh, if I play my cards right huh? From what I remember you asked me out, not the other way around." He was cocky, I could tell that already and it made him even more appealing. His whole swag screamed cocky, like he had no insecurities at all.

"I only said what you wanted to say but ya ass was too nervous." Shit, he got me there; my ass was scared as hell to even speak to him. If he hadn't asked, we damn sure wouldn't be here tonight.

"Yea, whatever. Where are we going?"

"Don't try to whatever me now cause I put you in the hot seat. Just be real, you wanted to ask a nigga out and was too shy, nervous or whatever. Right?" Storm looked at me as he asked and came to a stop at a red light.

Looking at him sideways with a slight smile, I decided to just be honest," Well yea, but I didn't think I'd see you again so, yea."

"Yea, I see we gonna have problems already," Storm responded with a laugh.

"What do you mean by that?" there was a confused look on my face.

"You'll see, I won't even have to tell you. Just wait and see." We pulled into a parking lot, and I recognized it as

Artie's Arcade. It had been years since I've been to this place because it was always packed and sometimes I hated being around crowds; it was also because I felt like I had outgrown an arcade. To my surprise, tonight the parking lot was near empty and there were only 2 other cars in the parking lot.

"What are we doing here? You have to pick somebody up or something?" I wasn't bourgeois at all, but this was not my idea of a date.

"Oh, you too good for the arcade?" he asked as he cut the engine.

"No, this is just not what I was expecting."

"I'm not a regular nigga and I don't do regular shit." That was all he said as he opened his door, walked around to my side and opened the door for me.

"Is it even open?"

"Yea, it's open." He grabbed my hand and helped me out of the car. The place we were at may not have been ideal, but he was being the perfect gentleman.

We walked to the arcade entrance and there was a man waiting there for us with the door open.

"Hey man," he greeted Storm with a smile. He was a short, older black man with a beer belly. They slapped each other up and then Storm directed his attention towards me.

"This is Skyy, Skyy this is Artie." Artie extended his hand to me and I accepted shaking it.

"Nice to meet you pretty girl. Now Storm, is this your girlfriend? If not, I may have to snatch her up for myself," he said with a hearty laugh.

"Nah, but she still doesn't want you old man," he responded shaking his head, while chuckling.

"You never know, she might have a thing for a man with a big belly. They say we keep them warm in the Winter." He laughed one of his hearty laughs again. "Just playing honey, anyway I'll be in the back if you need anything. Have fun." Artie turned around and headed to the back where I'm assuming his office was located.

Looking around the arcade, for the first time I realized that it was completely empty. Besides Artie, we were the only 2 in the building. Putting two and two together, it came to me that he must have had the owner shut down the arcade for just us tonight.

"Come on." Storm grabbed my hand and guided me towards the area where you could bowl. Like I said, this was a busy establishment. There were the vintage arcade games and then there were about 5 lanes where you could bowl as well. I remember Chi and I coming here for hours at a time.

"You know how to bowl?" he asked looking back at me.

"Not really, but I like to bowl."

"Well, let me bust ya ass real quick, and don't think I'm going to let you win because we're on a date."

"You don't have to go easy on me because I'm going to win fair and square." 30 minutes later and he had in fact whooped my ass in bowling. He showed me no mercy, and my score was trash compared to his.

"All that shit you was talking and now look at you," he laughed.

"No, I just took it easy on you because I didn't want to embarrass you by beating you on our first date," I tried to save face.

"Oh, word? You a clown, I beat you fair and square, as you called it. Don't be a sore loser now."

"I'm not, I'm just saying," I responded, laughing as I sat in the chair and bent down to take the bowling shoes off.

After they were both off, I handed them to him and he proceeded to go behind the counter and put them back in their respectable slots. It was kind of weird that we had the whole place to ourselves. It was really just us, and I had forgotten that Mr. Archie was even here. Storm came back from around the counter putting our shoes away, and asked me was I ready to get whooped in some games now.

I could see he was very competitive and he really wasn't going to just let me win, not even once. It was okay though because I may have been the pretty girl, but I could damn sure play some games. He had a rude awakening coming and he didn't even know it. Now he was bringing my competitive nature out of me.

For the next hour, we played games, and he won once but other than that, I killed him in all off them. We played Pac-Man, Donkey Kong and Galaga; some of the best old school games.

"So, you held out on me. You didn't tell me you were a game player," Storm said as we walked out of the arcade and into the parking lot.

"Just how you didn't tell me that you were in a bowling league," I joked. He held the door to his truck open and I hopped in.

"Well, I guess we both have some learning to do about each other," he continued with the conversation as he sat in the driver's seat and started the engine. "Where you want to go and eat at?"

"Wherever is fine."

"Let me know a place or we'll be eating from the Burger Shack fucking with me."

Thinking for a moment, I decided," Applebee's?" Yea, I know for a date most women would ask for something expensive, but I wasn't like most. Something good, quick and casual was good enough for me; I was already having fun. Storm had me feeling like a little kid.

20 minutes later, we were pulling into Applebee's parking lot and it was packed. I forgot that it was one of those late-night restaurants that were open late, so people were always here Friday and Saturday nights, like tonight. We walked in and to my surprise there wasn't a wait, so we were immediately seated at a booth near the window. As soon as we sat down, I immediately noticed the stares.

I know Chi said Storm was something like a local celebrity, but this was ridiculous. It had slipped my mind about his stature since we were at the empty arcade alone. Now being in a crowded place, it popped back into my mental. Instead of Storm being this down to earth dude, I was getting self-conscious and nervous all over again. Even though I shouldn't have, he had been a gentleman towards me all night.

"You'll get used to it," he spoke, and I looked at him realizing my eyes had been looking around us and his had been glued to mine.

"I'm sorry, I'm just not used to this." Shaking my head, I opened the menu to browse and see what I wanted.

"It's cool. If we decide to make things official just make sure you ready to handle the nosey bitches and niggas." He opened the menu as well and looked to see what he wanted. "What are you thinking about getting?"

"I was thinking the trio, where I can choose 3 appetizers. That's what I always get."

"I was thinking the same thing. You ever had the spinach artichoke dip?"

"Yes, it's great, I love it," I responded a little too happily. Food was one of my weaknesses; it was a miracle I still had a bomb figure.

"Yea, I see. Let me make sure I get that. Maybe it'll make me as happy as it makes you."

Laughing, I was about to respond when the waiter came to our table. To my surprise it was Quiana's friend Amiyah. I didn't even know the hoe had a job.

"Hey Storm, nice to see you again," she said smiling with her mouth and eyes. "And hey Skyy girl. I see you done snagged this nigga up for the night." Without responding, I just stared at her blankly until she got the point. She was wack as a bitch and she had one more time to say something slick. Amiyah was one of them hoes, you try to ignore because you know she just ghetto and dumb but at some point, you were going to snap.

"Ooookay, well can I get ya'll some drinks?" she asked as she popped her gum.

"I'll take a water with lemon."

"And I'll have the same thing," Storm ordered after me.

"Do ya'll know what ya wanna eat?" She was being so unprofessional and ghetto, it was killing me.

"Yes, can I have the trio with spinach artichoke dip, buffalo wings and the steak quesadilla."

"Okay and you handsome?" she directed towards Storm.

"I'd like the same thing. Great minds think alike," he commented looking right at me."

"Oh, ya'll just meant for each other huh? Anyway, imma go put ya'll order in and I'll be right back with drinks."

She turned and headed towards the kitchen and all I could do was shake my head.

"What you shaking ya head for?"

"Nothing." I wasn't mad at him because she had already hinted at fucking him and honestly, I didn't care. That was their business and who knows if that shit was true. Her trying to be funny and acting how she was, was just annoying. It damn sure wasn't going to mess up our date though.

"So, you go to school?" he asked.

"Well, I just graduated from high school and I'll be attending Nursing school in the fall."

"Cool. Where are you going to Nursing school at?"

"U of R."

"Oooo you got money," he laughed.

Laughing back, I responded," No, I just got a scholarship and graduated top of my class." He had the nerve, knowing he was like daddy Warbucks out here.

"Beauty and brains. I like that." Storm nodded his head up and down as he spoke. Amiyah walked over to the table and placed our waters in front of us.

"Ya'll food will be out in a minute," she stated then walked away twitching hard as hell, probably hoping he would look but he didn't bat an eye. She was trying way too hard and instead of me being bothered, I was actually amused.

We continued to talk and get to know each other. Chi had told me so much that she heard about him, but I didn't want to go by rumors. I wanted to know the man behind the money, the man behind who the streets knew. He let me in a little more than I expected.

He was 22 and hadn't finished school but was thinking about going back to get his GED and a degree. I told him I would be 18 in a month and he didn't have a problem with the age difference. This date was going smoother than I had thought, he was more down to earth that I thought as well.

He didn't talk about his dealings in the street or anything like that, but he let me in about his family. Storm and his mother were close, his father had died when he was young, so the memories were minimal. He asked about my family and I told him. My mother was cool, except for she was more of my friend than a mom and that I never knew who my dad was.

It was quite common for men to run out on women once they became pregnant but that wasn't the case. In my mother's line of work, she couldn't pinpoint who my father was, so she raised me the best way she could, the best she knew how. Sure, I used to ask about a father when I was younger, but then I got to the point where I just accepted it.

We talked even after we were done eating, after everyone else was out of the room.

"We're closing. Here go ya'll check and make sure you leave me a nice tip since ya'll took so damn long," Amiyah said as she placed the check on the table, still popping gum. She really was a piece of work. How do you want a tip but steady just talking and how do you ask for one?

Storm acted like he didn't hear anything as he opened the check, pulled his money out and grabbed the pen. On the check he wrote," Stop being a bird and maybe somebody will tip ya stank ass" with a smiley face.

"You ready?" he asked as he stood up from the table and reached out for my hand.

"Yep." Grabbing his hand, we walked out together looking like a couple. We got into his car and he started towards my house. It was a little disappointing that our night was coming to an end, but I had to go to work in the morning. Hopefully, he would want to go on another date. I was so consumed with my thoughts that I hadn't realized that he was staring at me.

"What?"

"Nothing, you just got all quiet and shit once we got in the car. What, you not ready to go home?"

Damn, it was like he kept reading my mind and knowing exactly what I wasn't saying.

"Honestly, I'm not but I have to work in the morning."

"What time you off tomorrow?"

"2:30"

"Iight cool, I'll come pick you up and we'll do something after. That's cool?" He asked while looking at me with the sexiest face.

"Yes, it is," I answered with a smile. For the rest of the ride, we just chilled and talked a little more. Once we got to my house, he walked me to my door and waited until I got in to walk away. Standing on the other side of the closed door, all I could do was smile. I mean, my grin was from ear to ear. My ass couldn't wait until tomorrow after work.

Chapter 3

Storm

It had been about a month and Skyy and I were still kicking it. It was something different about the chocolate beauty, something intriguing that I hadn't come across with anyone else. Yea, she was younger than most chicks I fucked with, but her ambition was crazy. She had goals, and you didn't see that a lot with some of these hood buggas that we had around our town.

"Umm yea, let me get a dozen of red roses and a dozen of white," I said to the lady at the flower shop.

"Must be one lucky lady," she responded with a smile.

"Yea, it's her birthday." Skyy was turning 18 today and I wanted to make her day special. She deserved to have the best birthday ever. All week it was the only thing she could talk about, so I knew she was excited.

The woman walked from behind the counter with the flowers in hand and that's when I noticed how stacked she was. Her face was average, but her body was something serious and yes, I was buying flowers for Skyy but I'm a man, I couldn't help but notice. She must have noticed me looking at her curves and in her mind, that gave her the green light.

"Are these for your mom, girl or your wife?" she asked as she handed me the flowers and ran her hand against mine.

"A friend." It wasn't a lie; Skyy and I were kicking it, but nothing was official yet. Hopefully it would be tonight.

"Oh, so that means that I can give you my number then huh?" Her head was cocked to the side as she asked the questions. She looked like she was in her upper 20's, usually around the age I went for because there was less drama.

"Imma be honest. These flowers not for my girl, but I'm trying to make her mine. You can give me ya number but I'm not making any promises to hit you."

Nodding her head, she replied," I can dig it, but if there's ever an itch that your "friend" can't or won't scratch, call." She was all up on me now, with the flowers being the only thing between us. Reaching into her back pocket, she pulled out a piece of paper with her name and number written on it.

Taking the number from her hand, I did an about face and walked out before things went farther. I could already tell she was the type I could have in the back of her shop bent over screaming my name out before she even knew my last. Getting into my truck, I pulled out my phone and checked the time. It was 1:00 and I had to pick up Skyy at 2:30.

She didn't know what I had planned for her, but I was ready to see her face when she saw the surprises that I had in store for her. Making a U-turn I headed in the direction of my right-hand man house. We needed to discuss some business before I got up with Skyy. His house was still in the hood; I kept telling this nigga we had money now and he didn't have to live here, but it was where he felt comfortable so whatever.

Going into my glove compartment, I pulled out my Glock 19 and concealed it in the waistband of my pants. Niggas knew who I was, but I still never wanted to be caught slipping. That was a mistake my father had made, and it sent him to an early grave. Chinx lived in an apartment building on Troup St. and it was always mad niggas chilling on the stoop and mad bitches clucking around the niggas.

"What's up man," I heard many greetings as I walked up to the building. It was 5 niggas sitting out here and although I didn't know their names, I had seen them around the hood. Shit, I won't even lie, I was bad as hell with names, but I could always remember a face.

"What's up ya'll? How ya'll living?"

"Cooling, cooling," was the general response.

"Iight, imma see you niggas on my way out." I walked inside the building and as usual the damn elevator was out of service. This nigga Chinx had the nerve to be on the 5th floor when he knew this shit was never working. Being a skinny nigga, this should have been easy for me, but I smoked more weed than a little bit, so that made this stairs shit a task.

Knock, knock

Reaching his door, I knocked and waited for him to answer. On the other side of the door, I could hear shuffling around.

Boom, boom, boom

"Nigga, hurry the fuck up!" As soon as the words left my mouth, the door flew open and a chick was walking out in a pair of short shorts, a crop tank top and sandals on. She slid past me and headed down the stairs while Chinx stood at the door with a royal blue Gucci robe on.

"Why you yelling and shit like you stupid nigga?" he asked as he turned around and headed into his apartment. "Make sure you take them damn shoes off to," he yelled back as he walked to his living room.

"Like I don't always do that shit?" Chinx said the same thing every time I came over. His crib may have been in the hood, but the inside looked like he was living in a luxury condo. His living room was all white, white carpet, white leather couches, tv stands, coffee table I mean everything. His house resembled Tommy's on Belly.

"Yea, whatever. But what's up?" he sat on the couch and sparked a blunt.

"Yo, I need you to check on shit today. I already handled the traps on the East, but I need you to slide through the West and check on shit there."

"Iight, cool. What ya ass got planned? You usually like checking on shit yourself, you know you an anal ass nigga."

"Pause. But I'm chilling with Skyy for her birthday and shit, so I'm not going to have time."

Chinx began to laugh uncontrollably and barely was able to pass the blunt to me because he was still laughing so hard.

"Fuck so funny?" I asked as I inhaled the smoke. Since I knew this nigga since grade school, I already knew what he was laughing at.

He finally stopped laughing enough to talk," Nothing man, ain't shit." Chinx was trying to brush it off as if that weak ass response he just gave me was going to rock.

Giving him a "yea right" face he knew I wasn't going to take that shit.

"Man, it's just I never seen you act like this with no female you ever talked to. You been open off of her and ain't even get a taste of the pussy. I just don't get it."

"That's what's wrong with the world now. Ya'll think you can't get to know someone before getting in their damn pants. Yea, I might be open, but shorty cool as a fan and she ain't nothing like these chicken head ass hoes out here."

"Well shit if you happy, I'm Gucci. You my nigga and I know you ain't gon hang ya player card up for just anybody. Shit, you probably still pulling bitches and getting numbers just in case shit don't work out." Now I was laughing. Chinx knew me like the back of his hand. We were damn near brothers, nah, we were brothers.

"See, I knew it." After getting blowed, making sure he knew exactly what to do and to make sure he let me know if there were any mishaps; I made my way out of his building and to go grab Skyy from work.

I got to her job in just the nick of time and she was coming out as I was pulling into the parking lot and up to the door. Getting out, I grabbed the flowers from the back and headed to the passenger side to open the door.

"Thank youuu," Skyy squealed and put her arms around my neck for a hug and gave me a kiss on the cheek.

"Dang, you two need to get a room." We parted and her friend Chiasia was standing there, arms crossed and a smile on her face.

"Man, shut yo ass up."

"Skyy, tell ya man don't be talking to me all stupid." Chi and I had grown closer and I was used to her little loud, ghetto ass, but you could tell she had a good heart.

"You started with us, and that's not my man."

"Oh, I wish ya'll would stop with that. You two are going to be so in love once ya'll stop playing and just be together."

"Man, mind ya business. Come on Skyy, let her ghetto ass get on the bus," I joked as I opened the door for her to get in.

"Oh, so now you got jokes but ya'll looking like the double mint twins." She was commenting on the fact that we both had buns in our hair.

"Fuck you, nah I'm just fucking with you. You want a ride home?"

"Nope, imma just get my ghetto ass on the bus," Chi responded as she walked away to the bus stop, sticking her middle finger up.

Laughing, I walked around to the driver's side and hopped in. Skyy already had her seat belt on and started asking questions as soon as I sat on the seat.

"Where are we going?"

"Hi, to you too. How was work?" I ignored her.

"Work was the same. Annoying and I watched the clock the whole time. Now, where are we going?" she asked with a smile.

Looking over at her I saw the gleam that was in her eyes. There was a sparkle that was always there; one of those special things I loved about her.

"Just chill out, we're going to enjoy our day and just go with the flow."

"Okayyyy," she said sadly, and I knew she didn't really want to wait. Skyy liked surprises but her ass was too nosey. Taking her phone out, she plugged the aux cord into it and started the music. Usually I wouldn't let her touch my radio because she always wanted to listen to those fake ass new rappers like Lil Uzi, 21 Savage, Young Thug and all those other niggas. Since it was her day though, I'd let her slide. She surprised me when I heard a song I put her on to blaring through the speakers.

These niggas prayed on my downfall

These niggas prayed on my downfall

On all ten, bitch I stood tall

Show these disloyal niggas how to ball

Go get a thermometer for the pot, I need this shit cooked

right

Let's keep this water 400 degrees Fahrenheit

You ever been inside a federal court room?

Nigga you ever went to trial and fought for your life?

Being broke did something to my spirit

Asked niggas to plug me, they act like they couldn't hear me

Look at me now, driving German engineering

You don't want your baby mama fucked, keep the ho from

near me

At the same time, I looked over at her, she looked
over at me and we both just laughed. She already knew what

I was thinking; I had put her ass on. Turning the radio up, I bobbed my head as we headed to our first destination.

Chapter 4

Storm

We got to the airport strip and immediately Skyy went to ask a question. I put my fingers up to my lips to silence her and it did.

"Go with the flow," I reminded her as I parked the truck and took the key out of the ignition. We got out and I lead her towards the fueled-up jet that was waiting for us.

"Good afternoon Mr. Castro."

"What's up?" I greeted the pilot. The jet wasn't mine, but I had used this company before, so they knew who I was. I wasn't one to play with my money like other fools buying shit they really didn't need. My black ass wasn't buying no jet.

"And hello you to too Miss," he greeted Skyy with a handshake.

"Skyy," she accepted his hand and shook it.

"Are you guys ready?"

"Yea."

"Yes, where are you taking us?" Skyy thought she was slick but I was smarter that than that. I had already told the company that this was a birthday surprise.

"You'll see when we get there, Happy Birthday." The pilot was on point and was definitely going to get an even bigger tip for that.

Rolling her eyes into her head, she got into the jet with me holding her hand. We got in, got settled and then finally we were off. As soon as we got into the hair, I pulled out my cigar box with an already rolled blunt. I was ready to get higher than we already were.

"Can you even smoke on here?"

"I paid for it, I can do whatever I want."

"You're so rude. What if that man has asthma, or what if it's against the rules?" She was throwing out questions left and right.

"Let me ask him. Yo!" I yelled out to the pilot. "You mind if I smoke this loud in here?"

"Oh my god." Skyy put her head down in embarrassment.

"Not at all Mr. Castro," he replied cool, calm and collective.

"Cool." Sitting back getting comfortable, I continued to smoke my l. Skyy looked at me and shook her head.

"Can't take you nowhere."

"Technically, you're not I'm taking you."

We chilled and vibed for the rest of the jet ride and after an hour we had reached our destination. I saw Skyy's eye light up once she realized that we were in NYC. She had expressed to me that she wanted to spend a weekend in NYC for her birthday, but she didn't have the funds. Of course, I offered to send her and Chi off, but she declined.

That was another thing that I liked about her. She didn't try to take advantage that I was a man with money. Skyy may not have had the dream job right now, but she was working on it and as long as that was the case I was willing to give her the world. Damn, she wasn't even my girl and had me thinking like this. A nigga had to be high.

"Ahhhh thank you, thank you, thank you!" she jumped in my lap and wrapped her hands around my neck again. Her ass was right on my dick and I had to think about something else, so my manhood wouldn't start poking.

"Damn girl, if I knew a day trip to NYC would have you like this I would have done it sooner."

"Shut the hell up Storm." Skyy hit me playfully on the chest and got off my lap. She looked down at me and bit her bottom lip; if I didn't know any better I would think she was trying to check my shit out.

The pilot landed and just as I had helped Skyy on, I helped her off. There was nothing, but a smile planted across her face as I led her to the car that was waiting for us. We had a driver because I hated driving in NYC; the only time I drove myself was when I came up here to handle business. Once we got in, the driver greeted us, and we headed to 5th avenue to start shopping. Her first birthday surprise was a shopping spree.

Our ride there was mostly quiet, she was looking out of the window taking in everything and again I decided to powder my lungs with loud. This time, she was so busy with the sights she didn't even comment on me embarrassing her by getting high in a "public" place. Turning my phone back on, I had text messages from Chinx. He was just updating me on everything I told him to, and let me know it went smoothly and he would see me tonight.

The other surprise for Skyy was a little surprise party at Carpe Diem tonight. She had never been to a club since she had just turned 18 and I wanted to be the first one she experienced it with. I was going to make sure it was done right with VIP, bottles and nothing but good vibes. Tonight, was going to be a good night.

After an hour of walking 5th Ave, Skyy finally found a store that she liked, H&M. We had gone past Gucci, Lord & Taylors even Saks and she wasn't feeling it. I honestly think she was worried about spending too much money even though I told her she could get whatever she wanted; I had a pocket full of money. We walked into the store and she immediately started going through the clothes racks.

The store was packed with women and some men sprinkled here and there. Skyy was in her glory as she picked out item after item and handed them to me. There were shirts, dresses, jeans, leggings, everything that you could think of, she was finding.

"Okay, now I need to try everything on."

"Iight, lead the way." Following her, hands full, we walked to the back of the store where the fitting rooms were. There was also a section to sit down, so while she went in and tried everything on I sat in the chair and scrolled through Facebook. Not one to be on social media like that, it was only used at times when I really, really wasn't doing shit and that was rare.

"Hey, stranger," I heard a voice and looked up. It was Yas and although she was looking fine, this was the last person I wanted to see while I was with Skyy. Moving my head to the side I looked towards the fitting room door, but Skyy wasn't there.

Yas was a chick that I messed with from time to time. Whenever I hit the city I usually hit up Yas and got with her. She was a cute light skinned woman, and her body was crazy. That was what I was most attracted to besides what she did with her mouth.

Nothing was exclusive with her, never had been and never would be. Sometimes she hinted on being more than just a fuck buddy, but I always shut that shit down. She had a lil name for herself in the streets, but I had never confronted her about anything, so she thought I didn't know. Honestly, I just didn't care.

"What's up?" I responded. I wanted to see what she wanted and get rid of her before any dumb shit could get started.

"Nothing, just doing some shopping," she replied holding up her arm with clothes hanging on it. "What are you doing here?"

"Iight, cool, cool," responding with a head nod, I was trying to avoid her other question. It wasn't really something I was trying to hide but it was none of her business.

"Okay. How long you going to be in town for?" she asked, and her face told it all. Yas wanted some dick and usually I would break her off but not today.

"Just for a couple hours yo then I'm heading back." Before she could get her next statement out, Skyy was heading out of the dressing room. Clothes still in her hand, but the load was a little lighter than when she had went in.

"So, I left a couple of things in there that just didn't look right on me," she said to me as she walked around Yas.

"Cool, so that's all you want? Or you need something else."

"Ummmm," she put her index finger to her lip, and looked around as if she was thinking if there was anything else she needed or wanted. Skyy didn't even get the chance to respond before Yas was butting into the conversation.

"Well since you're buying stuff, can I get my clothes paid for too?" she had her head cocked to the side.

"Oh, you know her?" Skyy asked with a confused look on her face. It was as if she didn't even see her standing there, she had paid her ass no mind.

"Yea, he knows me. Storm, you know her?" Now they were both looking at me, but sweat? That's what I wasn't going to do.

"Yas, ma, I was trying to get you away from me before Skyy even came out the fitting room, but you didn't get the hint. You out here shopping, cool, I'm not paying for shit and I'm not coming to see you. We gonna finish our day and you enjoy yours." Grabbing Skyy's hand we walked away, leaving Yas dumbfounded and to pay for her own shit.

Chapter 5

Chiasia

Pop a perky just to start up (pop it, pop it pop it)
Two cups of purple just to warm up (two cups, drank)
I heard your bitch she got that water
(Splash, drip, drip, woo, splash)

Slippery, 'scuse me, please me (please)

Arm up, or believe me, believe me (believe me)

Get beat, cause I'm flexin' 'Rari's (skrt)

You can bet on me (skr, skr)

Hey, hey, hey, tater tot

Fuck niggas on my radar watch (watchin')

Crocodile hunter, turn 'em to some gator shots (urr)

"Ayyeee," I yelled out as I twerked in the mirror in my panties and bra. My cousin Quiana and I were pregaming before Skyy's surprise party at Carpe Diem tonight. I had snuck into the 21 and over club before but tonight Storm had put us all on a list to make sure that we could get in. Carpe Diem was the hottest club in our town, and I couldn't wait to have some fun.

"Bitch you too lit," Quiana commented as she passed me the drink she had just made for me. We were drinking long island and Moscato mixed; it was a combination that was sure to turn us up.

"I'm just ready to have fun. It's summer and the only party I went to was yours. Other than that, all I've been doing is working." I took a sip of the drink, and my face scrunched up at the strong taste. This was going to be a good night, I could tell already.

Knock, knock, knock

There was a knock on Quiana's front door and she left the room to answer it. My makeup was already done, so I slid into my high waist shorts and put on my black Guess crop top. I wanted to wear heels as I usually did, but sandals would have to do tonight because I wanted to party without my feet hurting.

"Yea girl, we in here getting ready now," Quiana spoke as she walked back into the room with Amiyah.

"Hey girl. You look cute," Amiyah said to me.

"Thank you. What are you doing tonight?" I asked because she wasn't invited to the party, so I didn't know why she was here. Quiana was my plus one and Skyy told me about that shit she pulled on her date.

"I ain't got shit planned, so I guess I'm going to the party with ya'll."

"No, you're not. You and Skyy aren't even cool and Storm didn't invite you."

"Okay, and Storm didn't rent out the whole club just a measly ass VIP section. I can still come to that bitch and turn the fuck up."

"Yea, whatever. Just make sure you don't try to get in VIP because that will be shut down." I didn't like Amiyah, so I damn sure wasn't about to hold my breath and her ass knew not to act tough with me.

"Anywayyyyy, let's turn up." Quiana was trying to make it less awkward and she already knew if her friend said anything out the side of her mouth about my friend, there was going to be a fucking problem.

An hour later, we were pulling up to the club and the line was literally wrapped around the corner. Walking to the front of the club, I gave the bouncer my name and he opened the rope.

"What the fuck?" Amiyah was cut off by the bouncer, like I had said she wasn't invited and Quiana was my only plus one. That's what was on the list. I didn't even say anything as I looked back and turned back around to go into the party. She wasn't my friend, and I didn't feel bad.

The club was decorated in Skyy's favorite colors, black, white and gold. There were balloons covering the ceiling and there was a big banner that said happy birthday Skyy. Walking into VIP, he had the whole section rented out for just Skyy and her birthday. There were bottles on ice throughout the whole section varying from champagne to wine and liquor. Yea, this was going to be a good night.

Storm had gone all out for my girl and I couldn't wait for her to get here because I knew she was going to be surprised. There were a couple of people scattered in the VIP area while the main area of the club was packed. Quiana had waited by the door for Amiyah, so I took a seat by myself on the black leather couch. Pulling out my phone, I had a notification that Skyy was doing a Facebook live video.

I opened it and when I tell you my best friends face was beatttttt. Lawwwd, it looked like God himself had sprinkled that glow on her. She was lip syncing to a song I had never heard before, her and Storm were rapping together and looking like a power couple. They were looking like they were made for each other and I wished they would stop playing and just get together; that friend shit was getting old.

"You here for Skyy?" I looked up and it was Chinx talking to me. He was fine as hell, and even though he didn't know me; I definitely knew him.

"Yes, I am." Usually I had a witty comeback, but with him I didn't have shit else to say. The words were caught in my throat. He was standing here looking good as hell. Chinx had on a royal blue shirt that had a gold and white design on the front, a pair of all white pants, and a pair of white Giuseppe's on his feet with a gold chain hanging from the side.

His arms were decorated in tattoos and made the outfit look even better than it did. I usually wasn't attracted to light skinned guys, but Chinx was sexy as hell. He had the perfect mix of sexy and thug.

Licking his lips, he responded," Iight, cool. Have a drink, we also got some hookah going on over here," he pointed to a section where people were smoking hookah. "They should be here in a minute ma."

"Okay, thank you." He nodded his head at me and walked away. Taking a deep breath, I realized that I had been holding it the whole time he was standing there. That man was fine, and I needed to get on that.

Chapter 6

Skyy

Storm was really making this the best birthday ever. Everything was perfect, and I kept finding myself smiling from ear to ear. After shopping, we returned back in the jet, he took me home to get dressed while he went home and did the same. Now here we were, pulling up to club Carpe Diem.

We stopped right in the front and a dude I didn't recognize, retrieved the keys from Storm and hopped in the truck, I'm guessing to park it. He couldn't have worked there because there was no valet, and he was dressed in plain street clothes. Must have been one of his homeboys. Guiding me, hand in hand we walked through the front door and into the club.

I was shocked at how packed it was and then I noticed the décor. It was decorated in my favorite colors with a banner, balloons and all. Yea, Storm was showing the fuck out today. He slapped a few people up as we headed to the VIP section. As soon as I entered Chi, Quiana and Amiyah were the first faces I saw. 2 of them I was excited to see but that other one, I could have done without.

"Happy Birthdayyyyy!!" Chi screamed as she came up to me and hugged me like she hadn't saw me earlier at work. "I told that hoe stay out of VIP, but Quiana want to be Ms. Rogers and shit. She wants to be a damn good neighbor," she whispered in my ear.

Laughing, I responded," Thanks girl." Letting me go, she looked me up and down then started to go.

"You look mad nice. I see that shopping trip did you good. Did you get me something?" she joked.

"What you mean it did me good? He told you he was taking me?"

"Yea, he told me. The other day you were at the register with the old lady, taking forever; I asked him what he was getting you and told him that it better be good. Let him know you wasn't nothing like these other hoes out here, he better treat you right."

"Girl you so crazy."

"Dang, hiiiii," Quiana said from behind Chi. Her and Amiyah were still sitting there on the sofa. Honestly, I was trying to avoid Amiyah, just didn't feel like dealing with her shit today.

"Hey, Quiana. Thanks for coming," I replied as I gave her a one arm hug. Right in the nick of time, Storm came and grabbed my hand.

"Yo, come here." He grabbed me and walked over to the other section where it looked like him and his boys were chilling. The only person I recognized was Chinx. He was the only one Storm allowed me to meet before today.

Storm was different, I mean he was still the same person, but I got the softer side of him. The side that no one else got to see. He wasn't the gun toting thug when we were together, he was Storm. He was the man that made me smile like I was on top of the world.

"Aye, ya'll." Storm said to get their attention. The laughing and talking came to a halt and they all looked our way.

"This is Skyy, Skyy this my crew," he introduced us. There were scattered "hellos" and "happy birthdays" from the men in front of me.

I waved and said hi to them all and Storm whispered in my ear.

"Happy Birthday ma, and again you look good as hell tonight."

"Thank you," I responded with a smile on my face. As I walked back to where the girls were sitting, I could feel his eyes planted on me. This man had my insides melting tonight. He had already said it countless times how good I looked tonight.

My outfit for the night was an all-black jumpsuit. It was skin tight, but not too tight that I couldn't move. There was a slit in the front near my breast and there was also a dip in the back. On my feet, I was wearing a pair of royal blue heels and had a blue clutch as well. Yes, I wore heels today when I usually didn't, but I knew we had VIP so if my feet hurt there was guaranteed seating for me.

On our way to the club, Storm and I decided to make it official. So, we were officially dating and out of all my gifts, that was the best one. Storm was my man, my first real boyfriend. Other guys had asked me out, but they only made it to be my friend because I just couldn't get serious with the immature guys that went to school with me.

"Look at you all starry eyed," Chi broke my thoughts. Not even responding, I sat down next to her and poured myself a drink.

"So, are you and Storm together?" Amiyah asked and I immediately rolled my eyes.

Looking over at her, she had this stank look on her face. If her attitude wasn't so ugly and her actions so ghetto, she would actually be pretty.

"Why?" I asked. She was getting annoying, she acted like Storm was a thing of the past, but every time we were together and ran into her, it bothered her ass to death. Bitches loved to claim they were unbothered but every time they saw you, it just got under their skin. Amiyah was becoming the most unbothered, bothered hoe I knew.

"Oh, I'm just asking Skyy. You know he a hoe, I'm just looking out for you honey."

"Honey," I reiterated, "I don't need your help or for you to look out for me. Storm and I are good sweetheart and if we weren't that shouldn't even concern you." Directing my attention back to my glass, I took a sip. Today was my day, even though it was after 12 it was still my day, and that hating hoe was not about to ruin it.

"Hahahaha," Chi was dying laughing, and I know she had been waiting for me to go off on her. Amiyah didn't say anything else just sat back, with a stupid twisted look on her face.

"What you did for your birthday?" Quiana asked, trying to break the tension. I knew what she was doing, because that was her best friend, but Chi was her cousin, so she didn't want them to get into it. She would have been torn between the two.

Running down the list, I let her know about my day and knew that Amiyah's insides were boiling even more. Even if she fucked Storm, I know for a fact she didn't have him how I did. The surprised look on her face when she saw us at Applebees together and he didn't make any small talk with her proved that to me. Yea, I might have been young, but I was winning. The petty in me wanted to tell her yea, take that l baby.

It was 2 am and I was tired as hell. My party was a success, and I didn't have to say anything else to Amiyah. After hearing about my day with Storm, she went to the dance floor and bent over on any nigga she could get her hands on. Chi was going home with Quiana, so Storm guided me, holding my waist out of the club. The let out as we called it was crazy. There was double the amount of people that were in the club.

The truck was already pulled up in front and the guy from earlier handed Storm the keys. Even with all the chatter and people scattered around, the stares from the people standing around were noticeable. He opened the passenger door for me, and then walked around to his side. I could hear bitches on the street sounding thirsty and breaking their necks trying to say hi, and trying to get even a second of his attention.

Storm paid them no mind and got in the car. That was a good quality about him, he didn't pay attention or feed into the groupie shit. With his status, that was a good quality to have. He got into the driver's seat and immediately started the ignition.

"Put your seatbelt on," was all he said as he pulled into traffic, truck dispersing the crowd of people. Storm lit another blunt, smoked and then handed it to me.

"I don't smoke," I said to him, even though I knew he knew this.

"You don't smoke, or you just don't smoke with me?"

This confirmed that he did see when I hit Chi's blunt. Ever since the party, yea I did smoke. It was nothing heavy though, just here and there. I wasn't hiding it from Storm, but I wasn't about to be the chick that a nigga thought he was going to get high and drunk then fuck.

Taking the blunt from his hand, I told him," I smoke just not like that, and not all the time like you."

"I like what I like," he said as we came to a red light, but it changed almost instantly.

Handing the blunt to him, I started to talk," Thank you so much for making my birthday special. You really didn't have to, and I appreciate that."

Exhaling the smoke, Storm responded," It's cool. I know I didn't have to do it, but I wanted to. Are you going home or coming with me?"

The loud had my head cloudy and the sound of his voice had my juice box wet, but I wasn't ready to even go there with him yet. I didn't want my first time to be because I was high and horny.

"Home."

We smoked and talked until we pulled up in front of my house. All the lights were off except for the light coming from the TV in the living room. Storm got out of the truck, opened my door and walked me to the door. Our eye were low and as we looked at each other, we both smiled and started to laugh. Not a loud laugh, but a small one.

"I'm high as hell," he commented.

"Me too."

"What are you doing in the morning?"

"Nothing, I took the day off, so I'll be home."

"Iight, I'll be over in the morning. We can go do breakfast, cool?"

"Cool, I replied." He kissed me on the forehead and started back to the car. I, on the other hand opened the door and walked into the foyer. I took my shoes off and hung my key on the rack. My mother must have been in the living room since the TV was on. She had probably fell asleep, waiting up for me so she could talk my ear off.

Making a left, I turned into the living room and was shocked at what I saw. There was my mother, asleep on the couch but she wasn't alone. That wasn't even the big shocker. The big shocker is that there was Chiasia's father on the couch, holding my mother as she slept. They looked like 2 parents that fell asleep waiting up for their child to come home from her first date.

I was disgusted as I went into my room and closed the door. Just the way to end the perfect birthday, with my mother's whorish ways. My mother and I had a close relationship, and I loved her like crazy, but I hated what she did. The first time that I found out my mother had sex with men for money, I didn't talk to her for days; couldn't even look at her.

None of the kids at school knew about my mother because she only messed with clients that had money. They may have not been rich, but they made enough to live in the suburbs and drive the newest whips. Even though what she did was wrong, it wasn't close to home, so I always pushed it to the back of my mind.

This was different though. She was with my best friends married father. A man whom I looked up to and thought of as to be the perfect, family man. The kind of man

I wanted that you could be with and create memories with that man, and create a family. But here he and my mom were crashing that idea to the ground and then setting it on fire. Men were no good, he was an example of that. Now how and should I even tell my best friend?

Chapter 7

Skyy

The next morning, I was awakened by my phone vibrating under me. It was Storm saying that something came up, so he would have to cancel breakfast, but we could do dinner later. That was fine with me, so I could get more sleep. After texting him back, I rolled over and went back to sleep.

At least I tried before my phone went off again and again. The first one was from Storm saying come outside and the other was from Chiasia asking what I was doing. I decided to text her back when I got back in the house and threw on a pair of sweats to go and see what Storm wanted. He had just told me that he couldn't make it, so I was confused.

When I stepped outside, he was already out of the car waiting for me. As usual he looked good as hell and I took note of that.

"You were still sleep?" he asked as I reached him.

"Yea, I thought you were busy?"

"I am, but I wanted to stop and give you this." He handed me a handful of money.

"That's 5k, go out and go shopping or some shit today since I can't chill with you. Take Chi with you," he said.

"I can't take this," I attempted to hand the money back to him. "After all you did for me yesterday, I couldn't."

"You can, and you will. I know you like being independent or whatever but I'm ya man and imma give you shit all the time. It'll insult me if you don't take it," he put on the sexiest look and licked his bottom lip. "You're my girl so imma treat you like a queen, you deserve it. Now come on give me a hug and shit, I gotta go."

He took me into both of his arms, gave me a hug and just when I thought it was going to be the forehead kiss again, his lips touched mine and his tongue crept into mine. Storm's lips were so soft, and his tongue tasted sweet like he had just eaten a bowl of pineapples. Yes, the sweetness was that specific, he had to be eating pineapples. Finally, our tongues finished their dance, and we broke for air.

"Imma hit you later iight?" he said to me as we parted. All I could do was nod my head okay and head into the house. If just a kiss had me at a loss for words, I could just imagine what it would be like when I got the real thing.

Getting back into the house, I went directly into my room and put the money he had given me into my purse. I then grabbed my phone and texted Chi back. We made plans to go to the mall because her father was letting her borrow his car. Just the thought of her father made me cringe.

Two hours later, we were in the car heading to the mall. As we drove to the mall and talked about the previous night, we smoked and laughed at all the things that had happened. Chi also wanted me to put her on with Chinx. She was going on and on about the things she would do to him.

Chinx was fine, I could admit that, but he and Storm were opposites. Chinx was light skinned, where Storm's skin could be compared to midnight. Chinx had a brush cut and Storm had hair. Their attitudes were similar though, and you could tell that they were friends. Their whole street demeanor was the same.

"Skyy, are you listening to me?" Chi asked.

"Yea." I really hadn't been though. Once she mentioned Chinx, I started to think of Storm and my mind was stuck on him, so I started to half listen.

"Bitch, you weren't really listening to me. Lying for no reason," she stated as she made a right and pulled into the parking lot of the mall. The parking lot was packed, but that was common for a Saturday afternoon. After searching for not too long, surprisingly, we found a spot close to the entrance.

We both looked in the mirror at ourselves and gave each other a once over, then we both hopped out the car and walked to the entrance. The first place we hit was the cookie spot because we both had a sweet tooth. Eating while you shop was the best anyway. Chi and I went to almost every store in the mall, and she was too happy once she found out that Storm had given me money to pay for everything.

So, as we walked and talked through the mall, we browsed each store and bought whatever we wanted. Like me, Chiasia didn't care about any brand names so any store that had cute clothes were fine with us. 2 hours and countless bags later, we had put a dent into the stack of money and were now hungry. We decided to hit up a new Caribbean spot that was on the east.

The food at the new spot was great, everything from the oxtails down to the cabbage was good. After we were done eating, we decided to part ways. Chi had to get the car back to her parents and I had to start getting ready for my night with Storm. Speaking of Storm, I hadn't talked to him all day, so I decided to send him a text and see exactly what time we were getting up.

While waiting for his text, I decided to take a shower. Bringing my phone along, and turning on my music it looked like there was going to be a concert in the shower today. After singing along to Keyshia Cole and Monica, I washed up and got out. As soon as I was out of the shower and dried off, I picked up my phone to see if Storm had texted back.

There was still nothing from him which was strange since he always hit me back. Shrugging my shoulders, I figured that I would just watch TV and chill until he hit me back. CSI was on and this was one of my favorite shows, so I was all tuned in.

The blaring from the TV and the opening theme song woke me out of my sleep. It was pitch black outside of my window and looking at my phone made me aware that it was past 2 in the morning. I had no new messages or missed phone calls, so turning my TV off, I turned over and went back to sleep.

Chapter 8

Storm

"Arrghhh," I yawned as I woke up. Yesterday was a hectic ass day, so when I finally got home to sleep, it was well appreciated. The life of a hustler was a long, hard, never ending job but somebody had to do it. The only day I got to rest was Sunday, my favorite day of the week and that was today.

Getting out of bed, I went to the bathroom to pee, brush my teeth and wash my face. Walking back into my room, I went directly to my nightstand and checked my phones. First, I checked my business one to make sure there was no shit I had to worry about which there rarely was on a Sunday; then I checked my personal one. Besides the texts from Skyy, there was a message from Yas and a couple of other chicks.

The only person I was concerned with was Skyy as I began to write her back. She probably had an attitude with me because we were supposed to go to dinner last night but like I said; my day was hectic. 2 minutes after I had sent the text saying," Good morning," she texted me back saying that she was at work but would hit me when she was off.

Cool, I thought. With the spare time I had, I decided to hit back Yas and see what she wanted. Ever since she saw me at the store with Skyy she had been texting me, playing friendly never even mentioning it. That was her best bet though because we weren't together and that was the only time I was going to spare her feelings. I texted her a what's up and she responded immediately like she had been next to her phone waiting for me to respond.

She said she would be in town visiting this week and wanted to see if we could chill. Shaking my head, I sat on the edge of my bed and opened the drawer on my night stand. As I rolled up, I laughed to myself because these hoes were crazy. Just a couple of days ago, I had curved her ass in her face for another and here she was still basically inviting me to her pussy.

Breaking my thoughts, my phone started to ring and the Tupac song, "Dear Mama," let me know exactly who it was.

"Good morning old lady," I spoke into the phone as I licked the brown paper to seal the blunt.

"Boy, don't get beside yaself calling ya momma old. Now come and take me to the store so I can get dinner started."

"I'm on my way." We hung up and I hopped in the shower before throwing on a pair of black Nike sweats and a black shirt that had the logo Just Do It, across it in white. On my feet were a pair of grey, black and white 95 air maxes. In the process of getting dressed, I blew back.

This was my Sunday ritual. I went to pick up my mom; we would go grocery shopping and then I would chill and watch TV while she cooked. If I didn't see my mom any other day, she could expect me on Sunday. Pulling up to my mother's, I didn't even have to wait or give her a call before she was busting out of the screen door, like I had her waiting for forever.

Getting out of the driver's seat, I walked over to the passenger door and kissed my mother on the cheek before she got in. She was the one who taught me manners and if I didn't open this door for her to get in, I would never hear the end of it. Once she was in and settled, I closed the door and went back to the driver's side and got in. As soon as I pulled into traffic, my mother was starting in on me.

"I see ya eyes low, so you smoked that stank mess before I got in the car."

"Yes mom, I did." She hated the smell of smoke period and always complained about it. Sometimes I smoked in the car before she got in purposely, just to hear her bitch at me, but I wasn't in the mood to debate with her today.

Our grocery store run was smooth. Usually my mother was in there for forever, but she was in and out today. After taking the groceries in, I went into the living room, turned the TV on and got comfortable watching ESPN. My mother's pad was comfortable and every time I got here I instantly got sleepy.

It wasn't the same house I grew up in, it was actually an upgrade from where I had to grow up. She lived right outside of the city in a two level, 3-bedroom house. She didn't have many neighbors, and she loved the peace and quiet. It was your basic home, not too fancy; my mother was more of a plain jane.

Just as I looked down at my phone to check it, my mother walked into the living room.

"What's the name of the girl who has my son sprung. You been checking that damn phone since you picked me up." As I thought of it, she was right. Usually Skyy texted me throughout the day while she was at work, but she hadn't messaged me since earlier.

"Why you watching me?" I hit her back with a question.

"Don't sass ya momma. Move over," she said as she hit my arm motioning for me to move over. "Now who is she?" My mother always knew some shit without me having to tell her. Ever since I was young, she always did this. It was like she could look in my face and tell what was wrong or what was bothering me.

Not ever being one to lie to my mom, I told her all about the girl that had me "sprung." Also, not the one to have my mom all in my business, I told her some stuff but no real details. She would one day soon meet Skyy herself. My phone went off alerting me that I had a text, and I did. It was Yas sending me a question mark because I had never answered her earlier.

Silencing my phone, I looked back at my mom who was staring at me.

"So, I guess that's not Skyy it's one of your hoes huh?"

"Ma, they not hoes, just friendly young ladies," I joked putting my best Stevie J face on.

"Well don't bring Skyy to meet me yet. I only want to meet a woman that you're serious about and you're not serious until you're not entertaining anyone else." And with that, she walked back into the kitchen like she hadn't just dropped a jewel. Picking up my phone, I texted Yas back telling her that I could indeed see her this week.

There was a knock at the door, so I went to open it because I already knew who it was.

"What's up."

"What's up." Chinx and I greeted each other. Like I said, he was like my brother, so my mom was like his mom. We had been friends since we were younger. As I said, we didn't live in the most comfortable place growing up. We actually lived in the projects.

There were pissy hallways and drugs users littered throughout the jects and walking around in the middle of the night like zombies. Chinx's mom was one of those zombies and that's how we became so close. We were next door neighbors, and our mothers were friends. Rosetta was a nice woman before the drugs. She went to work and took care of home like most of the moms in the neighborhood.

Then Chinx's father left and from there she just fell apart. It was like she was in a constant state of depression that led from getting fired because she wasn't showing up for work and that led to her doing drugs. My mom tried to help her but when she continued to choose the streets over her son, my mother took Chinx in and let her do her own thing. It was cool to me because I now had someone to chill with 24/7.

"Yo, nigga what you watching?" Chinx asked as soon as he walked into the living room from saying hi to my mother and grabbed the remote. "The game on."

"Shit, I ain't know. What game?"

"Heat and Cavs." He turned the T.V channel and the sounds of the game started blaring through the surround sound system I had put into my mother's house; just for Sundays.

"Yo, what's up with ya girl friend?" He was asking about Chiasia.

"What about her?"

"Man stop playing. She a hoe?"

Ha ha ha ha ha

I was dying laughing. This nigga was funny, you know what bitches he was used to when he already asking if she was a hoe.

"Nigga, I don't know her hoe fax," and it was the truth. Shit, only hoe fax I cared about was Skyy's and I hadn't heard shit in these streets yet.

"Man, you know something. Shit, is Skyy a hoe?"

"What?"

"I'm just saying, you know birds of a feather flock together," he said with confidence, like this was a saying he lived by.

"Nah, she ain't a hoe. Well, I ain't heard shit."

"Oh, so she an undercover hoe?" he joked dying laughing. There was a lot of applause and cheers on the TV and when we looked they were showing a replay of Lebron hitting a 3 pointer in the last seconds before halftime.

"Anyway, how you know birds of a feather flock together? You must fuck with nothing but hoes?"

"Stop acting like you wasn't fucking them hoes with me. There was Monica and Jeronica, Toya and Tia, Lisa and Teresa," he stopped talking for a minute to think then continued," Oh, and those twins Tonya and LaRhonda."

He had a point, we always fucked with a pair of friends.

"I get it yo, I get it. Shut the fuck up now, you're starting to sound like a damn DMX song."

Chapter 9

Skyy

It had been 2 days, and I still hadn't reached out to Storm. He had called me a couple of times, but I just didn't feel like talking. It may have been immature to ignore him like this, but he broke our plans and then texted me the next day like nothing happened. There's no telling what he was doing when he was supposed to be spending time with me.

I know I shouldn't have been thinking like that but look at his stature. He was so known in these streets and I wasn't naïve. There were probably women at his doorstep ready to do whatever, whenever just to get some of his time. Then we weren't having sex and how could I expect a nigga like him to wait. Yea, this was a disaster waiting to happen.

It was my day off and I didn't have anything to do. I decided today might be the day to stop being stubborn and reach out to Storm, so that's what I did. I sent him a message saying good morning and waited for the response. A couple of minutes went by before my phone went off, but it wasn't him, it was Chi.

"Hello?"

"Yea, what are you doing?"

"Nothing, sitting here bored as hell. You at work, right?"

"Not anymore. I was there, and the fryer stopped working, so he let everybody leave."

"Oh okay. What you about to do?"

"I want to go to the movies and see that new Tupac movie that came out over the weekend. You trying to go?"

"Yea," I said just as I checked my phone and still I had no message from Storm.

"Okay, let me call my dad and see if I can take the car."

"Okay, text me and let me know." We hung up and down the hall I heard a phone ring and then the man down the hall answered. I couldn't hear exactly what was said, but I could imagine Chi bargaining with her dad, so she could use the car. Soon after the voice stopped, I got a message from Chi saying she would be to get me in an hour.

Chiasia really ended up taking 2 hours but she was always late for everything, so when she said an hour, I hadn't believed her. Storm still hadn't hit me back, so I chalked it up to he was just busy. Dudes are funny, they would be blowing your phone up then when you finally feel like talking they don't want to answer. Typical.

We reached the movie theater about 30 minutes before the movie was to start. It wasn't too packed probably because it was a Tuesday afternoon; so thankfully we had enough time to grab some snacks from the concession stand. Some people liked to sneak snacks into the theatre, but there was nothing like movie popcorn.

"Is that Storm?" Chi asked as she pointed over to the end of the concession stand. It was him and the girl from NYC. That was quick. He acted like she was being the most annoying chick at the store and here they were looking like a couple. So, this was why he hadn't answered the phone. I couldn't say that I was surprised though.

They were both decked out in all black and I was wondering if it was a coincidence or a his and hers kind of thing. They grabbed some napkins, and a straw then headed towards the Tupac showing. Turning back around, I looked at the menu to see what I wanted to get.

"Ummm, so you just gonna act like you didn't see that shit? Skyy, I know you don't like to start trouble or whatever, but after that party he threw you the last thing he should be is in a bitch face! Hell nah," Chi was talking to herself as she went to take her big hoop earrings out and put them in her purse.

"Chi, chill we not about to fight. I'm going to kill them with kindness and ignore his black ass. Don't trip."

We ordered our snacks and then headed into the theater. Looking around, even the movie wasn't too packed. I hated when you went to see a new movie and almost every seat was filled. It made me feel claustrophobic, there was a boundary when it came to my space.

We decided to sit on the top right where there were 3 seats. Chi and I always did that so our purses, jackets or whatever else could go in the middle. As we walked up the steps to get to our seat, we walked right past Storm on his date and he looked like a deer caught in headlights. Like he had just gotten caught with his hand in the cookie jar.

I gave him a little smile and kept going like we were nothing but mere acquaintances. The feel of his eyes burned a hole through the back of my head, and without looking back, I knew that he was watching me. We sat down and as soon as our asses touched the seats, Chi was talking shit but not loud enough that Storm and his date could hear.

"Bitch, you bugging! I would be over there acting all types of ignorant."

"Exactly, you would do that, but I'm not. I'm going to just chill and enjoy the movie, then when he wants to be all in my face, ignore his ass."

The movie was still showing the boring previews, not even the upcoming movies yet. Feeling my phone vibrate I took it out of my purse and it was a text from Storm. Looking up, I looked where he was sitting and realized he was now gone and just the girl was sitting there, head down in her phone. Swiping my phone open, the text from Storm immediately opened.

Him: Come to the hall.

Me: Wrong person

Him: Stop playing man. Come here.

Me: Nope

After sending the last message, I put my phone on silent and put it back in my purse. Before I could even get a handful of popcorn in my mouth, there was a hand wrapping around the nape of my neck.

"Bring ya ass in the hallway and stop playing with me man." He was so close, I could feel his lips to my ear and the smell of nacho chips on his breath. Dropping the popcorn back into the bag, I got up and followed behind him towards the hallway. As we walked past the aisle where his date was, she smacked her teeth but didn't make a scene.   We got into the hallway, but Storm kept going and we went to the women's bathroom. He turned around and locked the door before starting with the questions.

"Why the hell you been ignoring me?" he asked turning his hat from the front to the back. He was dressed in all black from his hat down to the Jordan's on his feet. The outfit was casual, cargo shorts and a shirt, but he made it look good as hell against his chocolate skin. "So, you don't hear me?"

Damn, get back into bitch mode, I told myself.

"Cause you're acting crazy. I wasn't ignoring you, I just got busy and I hit you today, but I see you had plans so that's why you were ignoring me."

"Nah, you never hit me," he replied holding his hand to chest, with emphasis on me.

"Yes, I did." I went to grab my phone from my back pocket when I realized I had left it in my purse. "I don't have it, but yea I hit you so don't act like you didn't get shit."

"Skyy, I ain't get shit. What you doing today?"

"Are you really trying to chill with me after your date? Don't insult me Storm."

"What you talking about? We can leave, this ain't shit," he said referring to the date.

"Boy, you wouldn't dare leave. Stop playing. That's guaranteed pussy in there for you."

"So, you think all a nigga care about is pussy? When I haven't even tried to fuck you?" He had a point there and instead of replying, I just rolled my eyes.

"Exactly. Go get ya shit so we can leave," he demanded."

"What? I wanted to see the movie, and I can't just leave Chi."

"What? She need a ride? How ya'll get here?" he was throwing out questions back to back.

"No, she has her dad's car, but I can't just leave her; I came here with her."

"Man, she not gonna care, tell her daddy said you gotta go. Imma go get the car, get your stuff and I'll be out front." Strom didn't even give me time to tell him no again, he just unlocked the door and left out of the bathroom.

Shaking my head, I washed my hands to waste time and looked in the mirror then proceeded to go get my things and tell my friend I was leaving. Hopefully, she didn't mind. When I went back into the theater, the movie was just about to start and there were more people than before. Storm's date was still sitting in the same spot, looking behind me towards the door. She was waiting for Storm, but little did she know, we were about to dip.

Sitting in my seat I leaned over to Chi, whom was all in her phone texting somebody and told her that I was leaving. She looked like she wanted to talk shit, but she just said bye and to text her later. I knew that when I did she was going to bite my head off.

"Where are we going?" We had been in the car for over 30 minutes and I didn't know where the hell Storm was taking me.

"Oh, now you want to talk to me?" I had been quiet the whole ride, but it wasn't like he had tried talking to me.

"You didn't try to talk to me."

"Yea, but usually you are talking, or commenting about something. You always have something to talk about." He was right once I was comfortable around someone I could talk for days.

"Well, nothing's wrong and I'm not ignoring you I'm just quiet. And if I was mad, I would have a reason to be Mr. I want to take bitches to the movies."

"That wasn't shit, I just felt bad for that girl."

"Okay, so imma feel bad for some nigga and let him take me to the movies. 2 can play that game."

"Do what you gotta do," he chuckled.

"Yep."

10 minutes later we pulled up to a nice suburban house. It was white with blue trim and a 2-car garage attached to the home. Storm pulled into the garage and closed it behind us, then came around to open my door.

"At least you haven't lost all your marbles," I commented just above a whisper. Yea, I was ready to be petty all day, so I hoped he was prepared.

"Skyy, shut ya ass up." He walked over to the house door, unlocked it and held it open for me. I walked in and was led right into the kitchen. The décor in the kitchen was black, red and white. Everything up to the rug on the floor in front of the kitchen sink matched; nothing was off, the red matched perfectly.

Following him more into the house, we were in a hallway that lead to a living room and steps that lead upstairs.

"Go ahead in there, imma go throw some shorts on, unless you wanna come up too?"

"Nope, I'm good. I'll stay down here and wait for you."

"You don't know what you're missing," he joked as he walked upstairs. Taking my shoes off, I lined them up where his other shoes were in the hall and went into the living room. It was all black with a black leather sectional that wrapped around almost the entire room. On the wall was a painting of him that was half black, half white with a gold crown on his head.

It was a nice picture, but a bit conceited if you asked me. Sitting on the couch, I took out my phone and browsed Facebook and Instagram while I waited for him to come downstairs. 5 minutes later, Storm was coming down the stairs with a cover, a box and some clothes.

"Here," he handed me the clothes. It was one of his shirts and a pair of new boxers. I could tell because there were the pack lines on them and they smelled like fresh cotton.

"What I need this for?"

"So, you can get comfortable. You wanted to watch movies, so that's what we about to do. Get comfortable and get high while we Netflix and chill. You can't get comfortable in them short ass jean shorts you wearing; you gonna throw them shits out too."

"No, I'm not. You're the one that bought them."

"Yea, and I see next time I got to treat you like a child and see clothes when you try them on because you obviously don't know what's appropriate to be wearing when you got a nigga."

"But it's okay to take a bitch on a date, that's appropriate? Yea, okay," I answered my own question. "Where's the bathroom?"

"Upstairs and take a left and yo," he looked at me and I looked back. "Make that ya last joke for the night."

Without saying anything, I rolled my eyes and headed upstairs.

"You can roll ya eyes all you want!" Storm yelled at my back.

The bathroom was nice. It was different from the other 2 rooms that I had seen. It was decorated a royal blue with cream and white. Of course, I didn't hesitate to look around the bathroom after the clothes he had given me were on.

After 2 minutes of looking through stuff, there was nothing strange in there, so I decided to just go back downstairs; after I looked in the master suite. Creeping down the hall like a thief in the night, I opened the door to Storm's room. His bed was big, I mean huge. It looked bigger than a king size and he had an entertainment center with a TV and surround sound system.

The room was decked out in gold and white. Even though each room was decorated different, I could tell he liked to keep them in the same color scheme.

"Skyy, you taking a shit or being nosey?" Storm yelled from the bottom of the stairs.

Creeping out of his room, I responded," Boy shut up. I'm coming now."

Chapter 10

Skyy

I woke up the next morning in unfamiliar surroundings. It took me a minute to realize where I was, but then last night came back to me. We watched 2 movies while we ate, chilled and laughed. Sometime while watching the 2nd movie must have been when I fell asleep, but I didn't remember coming upstairs.

Looking to the left of me, Storm was lying next to me still sleeping. Looking past his head, there was the alarm clock that read it was 6:26 am. Even though I didn't want to move I had to pee, and I couldn't wait. So, easing out of bed I tiptoed to the bathroom to relieve myself.

As soon as I was done wiping myself, the bathroom door was opening and in walked Storm.

"Good morning."

"Ummm, good morning." I was confused as he walked to the sink and started to brush his teeth as if I wasn't even standing there. The bathroom was always a private place for me and this was weird having someone come in and start doing stuff while I was in here, especially a man.

"What if I was in here shitting? You didn't even wait."

"Skyy, ya ass wouldn't be in here shitting. Trust me, I know."

"Whatever ugly." Standing up, I pulled up the boxers and walked to the sink to wash my hands. "Do you have an extra toothbrush?"

"Yea, here." He opened the medicine cabinet and there was an opened 5 pack toothbrushes with only 2 left.

After we brushed our teeth, Storm let me know he had things to do so he had to get dressed, but we could get something to eat. It sucked that he was so busy, but I understood. He was young and had to take care of himself; he also mentioned that he took care of his mom. After breakfast, Storm and I still wanted to spend time together. He had some running around to do, so he was taking me home to change clothes and then we would be on our way. We pulled up to my house and Chi's dad was creeping out of the side door. His suit jacket was over his arm and he was shutting the door with ease. Mr. Jacobs must have thought that I was home.

I had yet to confront my mom about the affair, but I could see that coming to an end today. Yes, I had been giving her the cold shoulder, but she didn't know why.

"Damn, ya mom a freak," Storm joked, but I ignored him and just got out the car. I wasn't mad at him at all, it was just the situation.

Going through the front door, I headed directly into my room. There was already an outfit that I had in mind. Since I had already showered at Storm's house, I slipped out of the clothes he gave me and slid into my pink, blue and black tie dye romper with a pair of tie dye PINK slides that matched exact. Changing my earrings, I took out my hoops and put in a pair of gold post and slid on my Alex and Ani bracelets.

Knock knock

Rolling my eyes in my head, I responded to the knock," Come in."

My mother walked into my room in a light pink, satin robe. Her eyes were low like she hadn't gotten any sleep and I definitely knew the reason why.

"Where are you going?"

"With Storm."

"Okayyy, where are you guys going?" she asked leaning on my dresser.

"I don't know." This is how our conversations had been going lately, short and sweet. What was I supposed to say to the women that was probably ruining my best friends parents' marriage?

"Skyy, what's going on with you? You've been really distant with me these past couple of days. Have you lost your virginity?"

Looking at her like she had 2 heads, I scrunched my face up before I replied," No, what does that have to do with anything?"

"When young girls lose their virginity, they start to think that they know it all, start smelling themselves. I'm just trying to see if that's what's going on here."

"No, I'm still a virgin mom." I looked in the mirror and applied mascara, lip gloss and eye liner. My hair was up into a ponytail. After doing a once over, I turned to my mother and let her know that I was about to go.

"So, are you going to tell me what's wrong?"

"It's nothing, mom," I responded as I walked to the door.

"Skyy!" she yelled, and I turned around with my hand on the door knob.

"What's the problem?" she asked. Our relationship had always been great. No matter what, I loved my mom and even though she did what she did to make money that was my mom. Up until this day, what she did had never interfered in our relationship. It's just that this was unacceptable, it was embarrassing actually.

"I want you to stop sleeping with Chi's dad." After saying that, I walked out of the door and I was on my way to chill with Storm.

Chapter 11

Storm

Ever since Skyy had gotten back in the car from changing her clothes, she was quiet as hell. I didn't know what was up, but her phone kept going off. All she did was silence it and continue to look out the window.

"What's up man?" I finally asked, as I turned down the radio. "That shit I said about ya mom was a joke." I didn't think she would take it serious, but maybe she was a little more protective over her mom.

"It's nothing, you didn't do anything to me." She was talking, but she was still looking out of the window.

"Something's wrong. Talk to me man, don't shut me out."

Skyy turned to look at me and when she did, there were tears in her eyes. Her beautiful, slanted eyes looked like pools of sadness.

"It's not that serious, I'm just taking it harder than I should."

"Well, what's up. I don't care if it's serious or not; you're crying so it's serious enough."

She went on to tell me about Chi's dad and her mom. The man that was sneaking out of the side of the house was her dad. Skyy told me how they were married and how her mother had a reputation of sleeping with men for money, but she'd never thought she would have sex with a man that was so close to them. She needed advice on if she should tell Chi. Skyy was her best friend and thought something like that should come from her, but it was like choosing Chi over her mom.

I told her what I thought, straight up, no sugar coating.

"Personally, I think you should just not worry about that shit. Chi is your friend, but that's your mom and those are 2 grown ass people that know what they're doing. I know it's like breaking a trust thing with your friend, but sometimes you have to just mind your business and let shit play out." I pulled into the lot of the jects and parked.

Normally, I wouldn't bring a female with me on runs had to do, shit, I never spent as much time with another woman, but Skyy and I had a good night and morning, and I didn't want that to end. It was nothing too serious today, just going around make sure shit was straight.

"But won't that be disloyal of me to know her dad is sleeping with my mom and not saying anything?" The tears had cleared up, but she was still just as emotional.

"Wouldn't it be an even bigger mess if Chi and her mother found out, and it comes from you? Let them find out on their own. Trust me a woman knows when her nigga is cheating. I'm about to go in there and handle something. I'll be right back." She nodded her head, and I reached into the glove compartment and grabbed my gun.

"Ummm, do I need protection sitting out here? Oh no, I thought you were doing normal running around, not drive-byes."

Laughing, I responded," Girl, I'm not doing no drive-byes. Just chill and lock the doors when I get out."

"And I need to lock the doors out here?" was the last thing I heard before I got out and closed the door. She was gonna be good, the most she had to worry about was these thirsty hoes trying to get a look in my truck. Nobody was going to fuck with her.

Going up the steps 2 at a time, I reached apartment C and knocked on the door. The door to apartment D opened and Candy stuck her head out. Candy was your typical hood rat. She was a thick lil something, light skinned with a flat stomach. Standing here in front of me she had on a pair of panties that were black and green with marijuana plants on them, and a sports bra on.

"Hey Storm. How have you been?"

"Wassup Candy, I'm good, you?"

"I'm fine, just how I look." The door to the trap opened, so I told her I would see her later and walked in.

There was a cloud of smoke as the door opened that came out of the apartment. Tank had opened the door for me and there was Biggs and Shotta sitting at the table. They were smoking and bagging up. Slapping them up, I walked deeper into the apartment and to the back where the money was.

It looked about right but I didn't have time to count it right now, so I would just do it later. Grabbing the black gym bag full of money, I left the apartment and headed to the truck. Skyy was sitting there looking at the door like she was waiting for me to come out. She was looking uncomfortable, and I hoped she didn't get all bourgeois on me.

Opening the trunk, I put the bag inside and started the walk around the car to get in the driver's seat, but then I heard my name being called.

"Storm!" I looked up and it was Candy, in her window looking down at me. "See you later," she said, biting her bottom lip. I just nodded my head and got into the car. From my peripheral, I could see Skyy staring a hole into me.

"What's up? You good?"

"I know you didn't bring me over here, so you could see one of your hoes."

"Skyy, are you serious?" She was starting to look real insecure and I didn't like an insecure woman at all. That was one of the reasons that I usually dealt with older chicks.

"Umm yea, you got Thotiana up there, about to break her neck to say see you later."

"Girl, that's fair play. Nobody messing with that girl. What type of nigga you think I am, imma bring you over a bitch house."

"Stop acting like you Mr. One-woman man."

Starting up the engine, I sat back in my seat before speaking," That shit from yesterday was just that, some shit from yesterday. Either you can get over it or you can't, and you don't have to comment over every bird that try to get with me. These hoes out here gonna be jealous of you because you're with me. So, are you with me or what?"

She hesitated a moment before answering, "Yea, but I'm still going to comment on what I want." Smiling, I turned up the radio and pulled back into traffic. This was going to be an interesting relationship.

Bzzzzz, Bzzzzz

My phone was vibrating, waking me out of my sleep. The first time, I ignored it but then it went off again. Reaching over, I grabbed my phone from the night stand; it was Skyy.

"Hello." The sound of sleep was evident in my voice.

"Hey, I'm sorry for waking you, can you come pick me up?" There was sadness in her voice and it sounded like she was on the verge of crying. The sound of her voice alerted me, waking me all the way up and I sat up in bed.

"Yo, you good? Where you at?"

"I'm walking down my street. Can you come get me?"

"On my way, hold on a second." Putting the phone down, I hopped out of bed and put on a pair of shorts and a shirt. I picked up the phone and she was still there; I also realized that it was 2 in the morning. "Yea, I'm leaving out the door now. We're staying on the phone until I get there."

"Okay, I'm sorry for waking you up."

"What you saying sorry for? It's cool. You need me, and I'm here." I was doing 80 miles per hour and talking to Skyy the whole time to her. When I pulled up, she was outside with a big pink duffle bag hanging from her shoulder. All she had on was a pair of pajama pants and a white tee.

Pulling up on her, I hopped out as soon as I stopped. Grabbing the bag out of her hand, I opened the door and waited for her to get in. Closing the door behind her, I walked around to the back seat and put her bag inside. When I got into the driver's side, I saw that Skyy was again, crying.

"You want to talk about it?"

She shook her head and responded," No, I just want to be with you."

"Cool."

2 hours later, Skyy and I were in bed and she was laying right up under me sound asleep. Once we got to my house, I asked her again what happened, and she told me that she had gotten into it with her mom about sleeping with Chi's dad. I had just told her earlier to mind her business, but she didn't listen. Women never listened.

Apparently, her and her mother had a big argument, and she told her to get out. It was different for me to care about a female this much. I would never have gotten out of my bed in the middle of the night if it was anyone else but Skyy was my baby, she was different.

I awoke to the smell of bacon being fried. When I opened my eyes, Skyy's spot was empty. Looking over at the clock, it was 7:30 and about time for me to start my day. My day consisted of getting out and making sure everything was running smoothly. It was the end of the month though, so it was reup time and that also meant that it was meeting day for my team.

After brushing my teeth and washing my face, I went downstairs in search of Skyy and the smell of the food that was filling the air. Walking into the kitchen, there she was in a pair of boy shorts and a small tee, flipping bacon and frying some eggs.

"Good morning."

"Good morning Storm. I made breakfast, that was the least I could do since you picked me up in the middle of the night."

"Didn't I tell you that was no problem," I responded as I walked up behind her and put my arms around her.

"Yea, but I still want to say thank you. Then you listened to me talk too for hours."

"You my lady, that's what I'm supposed to do." I grabbed a piece of cooked bacon off the plate and put one in my mouth.

"Are you ready to eat now?"

"Yea, I gotta eat and head out. What you got going on today?"

"I have to go up to my school and make sure my transcripts are sent for college, and then I'll be trying to find a place. I have some money saved up, so hopefully I can find something in my budget."

"Why you can't stay here?"

"You've already did enough, and I don't want to impose."

"Skyy, you bugging, you're staying here. I'm not about to have you out looking for a place when I have 2 extra bedrooms upstairs." Yea, it was kind of early for her to be moving in, but it was what was needed at this time and I didn't mind.

"No, I really can't Storm. I opened my big mouth and now I have to face the consequences. So, I'll be going to find a place. Just give me about a week or so and I'll be out."

I nodded my head up and down, but little did she know she wasn't going anywhere.

Chapter 12

Skyy

1 week later and I finally found a low-key spot that was downtown. Surprisingly, it was in my budget and was actually a nice studio, so I was elated. It was a really big room, so I still had room even though it was only one area. My kitchen had a black and white island that separated it from my big area. Storm paid for all my furniture, I didn't

want him to, but his crazy ass said it was either that or living with him. Since it was a studio, I didn't really need too much anyway.

Chi was coming over today to help me decorate. Storm had movers move everything in so now it was just decorating everything and making the room match my personality. I still hadn't told Chi why I moved out. All she knew was that me and my mom got into it and she kicked me out. I know it was weird to her because my mom and I were so close, but I still couldn't bring myself to tell her why.

Buzzzz

The door buzzed and going over by the intercom, I hit the button to let Chi in. 2 minutes later she was knocking on the door, but it was already unlocked for her.

"It's open!" I yelled.

"Ohhhh, I like," Chi said loudly as she walked in wearing a pair of blue and white tie dye flare pants and a white crop top. She took her flip flops off at the door and joined me on the floor. I had everything set out in front of me.

"You want me to give you a grand tour?" I asked being dramatic.

"Girl, a tour? It's only one room."

"I know, I was just going to stand up and spin in a circle."

"Soooo, we haven't really talked since you left the movies that day."

Thinking about it, we hadn't. From the drama with my mom, looking for a place, working and chilling with Storm I realized we hadn't talked all week and that was rare. We usually talked every day.

"Oh shit, I really haven't talked to you." While we got my place together, I ran down to her about everything that's been going on; without going into details about my argument with my mother. Then I got to the good part, the part that I knew she wanted to hear.

"So, the other day Storm and I were talking, and he said that Chinx wants to get to know you. Apparently, he asked about you and wanted to know if he could get your number."

As soon as the name Chinx left my mouth, she was smiling ear to ear, so I already knew it was okay.

"Hell yea, you can give it to him!" she said a little too enthusiastically.

"Trust me, the way you were staring at him and flirting with him at my party; I knew you wouldn't mind so I already gave it to him."

"Well, when did you give it to him? He hasn't called yet, I don't think," she said as she looked in her phone and checked her call log I assume.

"Girl, he probably didn't call yet. Storm's been busy, so he probably has too."

Throwing her phone to the side, she had a sad look on her face like she was so disappointed.

"I'm hungry. I don't get any snacks for helping you do this?"

"Chi, you just got here, and I didn't even go grocery shopping yet," I said with a laugh.

"Well, can we order something? The least you can do is feed me."

Shaking my head, I got up and went over to the island in the kitchen. A Chinese place down the street had mailed out menus and it was my first piece of mail. We ordered and while we waited for the food, I got Chi to at least do some work instead of just talking my ear off. An hour into decorating the food was eaten, and we were about halfway done.

My phone vibrated, and it was a text from Storm. He asked me how the apartment was coming along and if I needed anything else. Texting him back, I let him know that I was fine and Chi and I were taking a break eating. Storm let me know he wouldn't be able to stop by later like we originally had planned, but tomorrow we would be able to spend the day together. Even though it wasn't ideal, it was fine because I needed to finish getting my place together.

2 hours later and finally everything was put where I needed and wanted it to be. My living room area was decorated hot pink and black, while my bedroom area was black and red. Even though it was different colors the black helped everything mesh together. There were quotes on the wall and my name spelled out in some bejeweled wooden letters. It might have been a bit childish but to me it was cute.

"Ohhhh, we should go over to Froggers tonight!" Chi, jumped up on the couch and said to me like she just had the brightest idea.

"How the hell are we getting into Froggers?" It was a bar that was over on the east side of town, but of course we were not 21 and over. How did she expect us to get into Froggers?

"I know somebody who works at the door. Let me see if he's working tonight." She picked up her phone and her fingers went to moving as she tried to get us plans for tonight.

"Who do you know that works security there?"

"Remember that guy I met at work? The one that works doing construction?"

"Oh, the old guy," I commented as I remembered the older man that came into our job a couple of weeks ago.

"He said yes, and for your information, he's only 28."

"Old enough."

"Whatever, do you want to go or not?"

Thinking about it, I figured why not? There was nothing else for me to do but sit in the house and look at the four walls.

"Yea, I guess."

"Mmhmm, get up and get dressed so we can go. I

have my dad's car." Just the mention of her dad made me roll my eyes.

"What was that for?"

"Nothing, just thinking about what I'm going to wear since I have no clothes," I lied.

"No, no, no, we are not doing that today. Let me look for something because you always want to pull that shit knowing you have clothes." While she raided my closet, I went to the bathroom, so I could prep my face for makeup and take a shower.

When I finally came out of the bathroom, Chi had an outfit laid out for me. It was actually cute, so I didn't even complain as I got dressed. It was a pair of satin powder pink shorts and a spaghetti strap top that matched with it. For my shoes, she laid out a pair of powder pink PUMA Rihanna fur slides. Chi was wearing what she already had on, so she was just waiting for me to get ready.

I don't usually do this unless I'm drunk or I'm high

But I'm both right now, got me talking about my life

I don't usually do this unless I'm drunk or I'm high

But I'm both right now

I don't usually do this unless I'm drunk or I'm high

But I'm both right now and I need ya in my life

I don't usually do this unless I'm drunk or I'm high

But I'm both right now

Yeah, I'm both

Yeah, I had a drink, yeah I smoked

Yeah, you think I need you, but I don't

Just left out Dubai with all my folk

Open water, my location is remote

Shout out Yachty but this ain't a lil boat

This some shit I wrote up back when I was broke

We walked into the bar and the music was playing
from the juke box. I had never been to a bar of course, so this

was different. I was taking everything in, the crowd, the music, everything. There was a dart board when we first came in that was empty. Chi said she had played with her cousin and her friends before and said it was too fun, especially once you had a drink.

We both ordered vodkas and cranberry's and played a game of darts. It wasn't that packed, and I was grateful for that because I hated to be around a crowd of people. After 2 games, we decided to sit and chill for a minute. As soon as I sat down, 2 people walked through the door and when I say my face hit the floor, it hit the floor.

There was none other than Storm, he was with the same chick from the movies and he damn sure didn't look as busy as he said he was. She was dressed in an all red skin tight, halter dress. Her hair was long, almost down to her ass and she had a pair of red bottoms on her feet. The Birkin bag on her shoulder was red as well. Storm was looking good too. He was wearing white and gold with his chains glistening looking like he had just stepped off the cover of GQ.

I wasn't feeling it at all and the strong drink that I had wasn't making it any better. Storm was proving to me that he wasn't shit time and time again. Instead of being subtle like I was last time, I decided to just act ignorant. Fuck it, fuck shit up and leave.

He hadn't even noticed me when he came in. They walked right past me and Chi and headed to the bar. I wasted no time walking up to them and Chi was right behind me. Storm was standing next to her and ordering their drinks while she was holding on to his arm, basically glued to his side, looking like she was his trophy wife.

"Funny seeing you here." Storm turned around at the sound of my voice and his eyes met mine.

"It's not even what it looks like," he immediately said trying to cover up what I could clearly see with my eyes.

"So, what is it like, because to me it looks like this is your girlfriend and I must obviously be your side piece."

"Come on," Storm grabbed my hand to lead me away from the woman in the red dress but that wasn't happening today.

Yanking my hand away from him, I turned to her and introduced myself," Hey, I'm Skyy and you are?"

"Yas."

"Cool. You guys have fun." Heading out the door, I didn't look back as me and Chi left. We pulled out of the parking lot and my phone started to ring. Without even looking at it, I knew who it was. I ignored it and added him to my block list. This was the last straw. He was not for me, I didn't deal with community dick niggas.

Chapter 13

Storm

2 months later

"Goddamn." I woke up feeling like the jaws of life was taking my soul from my body through my dick. This woman had some kind of super power when it came to giving head. My eyes were still closed, but I pushed the back of her head until I felt the tip of my dick touch her tonsils.

Slurp, slurp, slurp

Yas always gave me great head, and that was partially the reason that I kept coming back. Her pussy was alright, I won't front but that head. Mannnn whenever I thought about it my mouth started to salivate as if I was thinking about salt and vinegar chips. I finally opened my eyes, and she was bent over on the bed, dick in her mouth with her back arched and ass in the air.

5 minutes later, my cum was going down her throat and she swallowed every drop. Looking up at me she wiped her mouth with the back of her hand and then got out of the bed and went into the bathroom. Picking up my phone off the

nightstand next to her bed, I checked the time, and it was time for me to get on the road.

"Damn, that shit too hot," I flinched as Yas started to clean me off with a towel.

"Oops, sorry."

"Man, you trying to burn my damn dick off."

"I said sorry Storm damn. You're always complaining, be appreciative I woke your ass up with head when you know I have bad ass morning sickness."

"Yea, cool. Let me get up, I have to go anyway," I sat up on the bed and turned until my legs were hitting the floor.

"You're leaving now? This early in the morning? We can't go to breakfast first?" she asked with a pout. "The baby's hungry."

"Nah, I can give you money to eat but I gotta go." Without waiting for a reply or for her to whine some more, I got up and walked into the bathroom and closed the door. My ass needed to shower and be out.

On my way back to the Roc, my mind drifted to Skyy as it usually did. Ever since that night she saw me with Yas, she hadn't answered a call or text. After a week, I figured she had cooled off and if not oh well, we still had to talk but when I went to her apartment it was cleaned out. Her next-door neighbor said she had moved but didn't know exactly where she had moved to.

Chi and Chinx had been chilling and of course I tried to get some info from her, but all she said was that she was doing okay and didn't want to talk to me. Skyy didn't work at the Burger Shack anymore either, it was almost like she had fell off the face of the Earth. After trying everything and still not being able to get in touch with her, I decided to say fuck it. I had never chased a bitch in my life and she was reminding me why.

Now back to that night, the only reason I was there with Yas was because she kept hounding me after the movies saying she had to tell me some shit. I picked the bar because it was usually low key, but low and behold there was Skyy and Chi. Anyway, Yas told me she was pregnant and that it was mine, but I didn't believe that shit. She said she was already 13 weeks and would have to have surgical abortion, so she wasn't with it.

In my mind, I didn't have a baby on the way until there was a paternity test done. Nobody but Chinx knew that she was pregnant, not even my momma and nobody was going to know until there was proof. Until then, she kept me updated on the pregnancy and I came to the city as much as I could. Her ass was honestly starting to get on my nerves though and clingy as hell.

"Momma!" I yelled as I walked into the house. It was Sunday and that was why I had to leave Yas so early.

"I'm in here!" she yelled from the kitchen. Walking into the kitchen, my mother had her slow jams playing while she swayed back and forth to the music.

"Momma what you in here doing and what you know about this music?"

"Boy, this music is before ya time. I had ya daddy singing this to me back in the day," she said swaying even harder.

Girl, you know I love you

No matter what you do

And I hope you understand me

Every word I say is true, 'cause I love you'

Baby, I'm thinkin' of you

Tryin' to be more of a man for you

And I don't have much of riches

But we gonna see it through, 'cause I love you

"Yea, okay. I heard through these streets you were running after my daddy," I joked.

"That's a damn lie and you know it. Now who pregnant?"

Her question shocked me and if her back wasn't turned to me, she would see it all over my face. I looked like a kid caught stealing out of the cookie jar.

"I had a dream about fish, and I know I'm not pregnant, so it must be you or Chinx that got one of these tramps pregnant."

Letting go of the breath I was holding onto, I let her know that I didn't have anyone pregnant and she was better off asking Chinx about that. She took my answer, and I went into the living room to chill and make sure I was not in the line of fire.

"Nigga, get up." I had fell asleep and this nigga Chinx was waking me up.

"Man, what?"

"Why the hell you got momma asking me if I got somebody pregnant?"

"I don't have her asking nothing. She asked me, and I told her hall nah, I ain't got no baby on the way; but I never said you did."

"Yea, whatever man. When you gonna tell her about Yas and the baby?" he asked as she sat down.

"When that DNA test comes back and says it's mine."

"Cool." Chinx had his phone out and was no longer paying me any mind. I already knew who it was Chi. That nigga said he would never be feeling a chick, but his ass was feeling her.

"Ask her how Skyy is?"

"Ha ha ha ha, what? I thought you said you was done chasing over her ass." He was laughing like he just heard the funniest shit of the day.

"Bruh, just ask her." Chi said she was doing good, started school but she still didn't want to talk to me.

"Cool," I responded.

As much shit as I had talked, here I was outside of Skyy's school waiting for her to come out. I knew a lady that worked in administration and was able to pay her a few dollars to get Skyy's schedule. Looking at the time, she was set to get out in another 5 minutes.

By the time she came out, I was leaning against the driver's side door, roses in hand and a gift I had gotten for her as well. She walked out in a sundress that I had bought for her with a pair of sandals on. Looking good as hell, I would have been licking my lips, but she wasn't alone. There was some light skin nigga next to her and they were walking and laughing together. She was so much into the conversation that she hadn't noticed me yet.

When we finally linked eyes, the smiles from her face was gone but instead of walking past me like she didn't know me; she said bye to her friend and walked over to my truck.

"What are you doing here?"

"I came to see you and see what's up. Can I take you to lunch?" She was hesitant, and I could see it all over her face. "I just wanna talk to you."

Finally, she nodded her head yes and I opened the door so that she could get in. The ride was quiet, and she didn't even open the gift that I had gotten her. Shorty really wasn't feeling me.

"You're not going to open what I got you?"

"Not right now."

I didn't even say anything as we pulled into the parking lot of the Jamaican spot I remembered she said she liked. Opening her door, we went in, ordered our food and found a spot in the back near the window. There were people throughout the restaurant, but it wasn't too packed either.

"So, what's up?" Skyy asked as she put a forkful of food in her mouth.

"You too good to open my gift, but you not too good to eat that food huh?"

"You asked me here, I was fine where I was going."

"And where was that?" I asked because I knew what she was hinting at. The way she was smiling at that light skinned nigga was the same way she used to smile at me.

"With my friend."

"What friend?" This wasn't what I had brought her here for, but now she was starting to piss me off.

"Nobody, just a friend from school. Why are you questioning me? Don't you have a whole bitch?"

"Cool, let's wrap this shit up so I can drop you off." Getting up, I grabbed 2 to go containers so that we could wrap up our food and go. When I got back to the table, I handed her hers and started packing mine up.

"So, we're leaving?" Skyy asked with a confused look on her face.

"Hell yea. I'm not about to keep kissing your ass and you talking about your "friend." Get the fuck out of here with that shit." She wasn't moving quick enough, so I grabbed her plate and fork and started putting her food in the container for her. Fuck that, I was being way too damn nice and she had me fucked up.

"Come on." I got up and headed to the truck. Wasn't no holding any doors, no nothing. She could do that shit herself. As soon as her ass hit the sit, I backed out of the spot and sped back to the school, so she could get her car. I didn't even wait until she got to her car just sped off, without looking back.

Skyy had me fucked up. The gift I had given her I grabbed off the arm rest and put it in the glove compartment. I could give that shit to Yas because I knew she would appreciate it. Her young ass had me feeling her, but I was done. There was no more trying to explain. She could go ahead about her business and I would do the same.

Chapter 14

Skyy

After Storm blew up on me, honestly, I was in shock. He had never so much as gotten mad at me, but it was funny that the mere mention of another guy had steam coming out of his ears. Chi had been telling me that Storm had been asking about me for the past couple of weeks, but I didn't care. He had been caught not once, but twice with his hand inside of the cookie jar. Now it had been about 2 weeks and Chi said he hadn't asked about me not once.

"What are you over there thinking about?" Lou asked breaking my thoughts. Lou was the friend that Storm saw me with when he showed up to my school. We had been hanging out lately. He was in school to be a traveling nurse, and we had a class together. When he first approached me, I didn't take him serious because he wasn't my type; but his personality outshined that and he wasn't ugly just wasn't chocolate like I preferred.

"Nothing, just thinking about that test I have on Monday. This will be my last day out of the house because I will be hitting the books all weekend."

"Well, thank you for letting me take you out tonight," Lou said with a smile as he grabbed my hand and kissed the top of it. That was another thing, he was so sweet and affectionate.

Blushing, I smiled and replied," Of course." We were headed to the movies and then as I said I would be hibernating all weekend, studying my ass off.

2 hours later, the movie was over, and we were walking out of the theater arm in arm when we bumped into Chi and Chinx. They were walking in as we were walking out.

"Skyyyy." Chi was being her usual loud self.

"Hey Chi, hi Chinx." He nodded his head in response and put his head back down into his phone. I didn't expect anything more. Storm was his friend, so of course he wasn't about to be all cool with me or my date, and that was fine.

"Hi, I'm Chi and you are?" she stuck her hand out to introduce herself.

"Lou," he took her hand and shook it.

"Well, I'll call you later, or it might be in the morning," she said as she looked back at Chinx. Her ass was so damn nasty because I knew right where her mind was at.

We said our farewells and Lou, and I headed to his car, so he could take me home. I needed to get some much-needed rest tonight. Like the gentleman he was, he pulled up right in front of my building and opened the door for me. That was one of the ways that he was similar to Storm, well before he acted ignorant. He always made sure to open the car door for me.

Other than that, though total opposites. As I looked at him decked out in a blue and white plaid shirt, a pair of khakis and a pair of loafers on his feet, I could definitely tell the difference. Storm was always in some hood shit, but he made it look so good.

"Have a nice night. I'll call you in the morning," Lou said as he hugged me and then held my building door for me until I got in. I said hello to the doorman and got on the elevator to the 6th floor. Originally, I was on the 4th floor, but once Storm and I broke up I made sure to move my place because I knew he would be popping up.

Getting off of the elevator, I turned towards my apartment and felt like I was smacked in my face. There was Storm standing outside of my door, arms crossed, looking in my direction. He looked like he had been waiting for me and it wasn't for a good reason.

Walking up to him, I tried to keep my voice down," How did you know where I live and what are you doing here?" Putting the key into the door I opened it, so we could go in. The way he acted the last time we saw each other was bad and I didn't know how he would act tonight.

"I got my ways. Where you was at?"

"Out." Taking my shoes off, I was about to drop my clutch on the island and take a seat on the couch when I felt myself being pulled back. Storm had grabbed me by the hood on the jacket that I was wearing.

Pulling me back into his arms, he got in my ear and spoke," Skyy, stop playing with me. Where were you at?" I could smell the weed on his clothes and there was the smell of mint on his breath. The sound of his voice made my pussy get a feeling where I had to squeeze my thighs together.

"Get off me." I pulled his hands from around me and walked to the island, but he was right up on me.

"You were with that nigga weren't you?" His dick was now pushed up against my ass with his body towering over me. Both hands were placed on each side of me on the island.

"You already know that. That's why you're here isn't it?" Chinx must have told him that he seen us at the theater and this asshole decided to do a popup.

Backing up from me he turned me around to face him. That's when I noticed just how red and low his eyes were. He looked at me like he had so much to say, but he didn't know where to start. Looking at him, I waited for him to say something, but he never did.

"What is it?" I asked.

"A lot. What's up man? Why you going on dates and shit when you know you don't want that nigga? You want me."

"What makes you think I want you? A man that cheats on me and keeps lying." I rolled my eyes.

"You never gave me a chance to explain. Come here man." He grabbed my hand and guided me over to the couch. We took a seat, and he took a deep breath before he started to speak.

"I never cheated on you. Yea, you saw me at the movies and the bar with shorty, but I didn't do anything with her. That movies shit wasn't about nothing; you see who I left with. Skyy, you have to realize I've never been in a relationship before, so some shit you gotta work with me on. That bar shit, she just wanted to talk, and I was trying to pick a low-key spot to talk to her at. What? You'd rather her at my shit?"

He paused, waiting for my answer.

"No, but.."

"Exactly." He blurted out before I could even finish what I was saying. "Imma always keep it real with you and from here on out, I can promise you that. You're who I want to be with, but just let me know right now either you with it or you not. I'm not into chasing after a female, so this cat and mouse shit has to stop."

I didn't know what to say; I was at a loss for words. Should I believe him, or should I let this relationship go? Lou seemed like a good guy and he was putting in the effort, while here there was a man telling me that I would have to work with him and that he wasn't about to chase me. But wasn't a relationship all about the work? If he wasn't going to chase me, then did he really even want to be with me?

"Yea." It came out before I even had time to evaluate everything; before I thought of all my options. Storm did something to me though, and that I couldn't deny.

"Come on, let's go take a shower so we can go to sleep. A nigga tired."

"I can take a shower alone. Go ahead and take yours, then I'll take mine. We're back together, but I'm not letting you off that easy."

"Skyy, how many times do I have to tell you stop playing with me?" Grabbing my hand, he pulled me to the bathroom. Storm started the shower and then proceeded to take his clothes off. This was my first time seeing him naked. Anytime we were together he had on at least boxers.

Once he noticed I wasn't taking anything off and was just standing there, with my jacket still on and all; he turned around and started to unzip my jacket and take everything off. In any other instance, I wouldn't have been standing here frozen, but his dick was in my view and I couldn't help but stare. Since my treasure had never been touched, I had never seen a man naked, but Chi had told me about her sex stories.

From what she told me, men lied about being so heavily endowed and were anything but. They would say they could fit Magnums when they really should just stick to Lifestyles. Storm was on a different level, and all I could think was where was he putting that? Storm had been blessed. His dick was just as chocolate as him, big with a slight curve.

"You good?" he asked while looking at me with a smile, and I realized that I was now just as naked as him.

"Yea." Taking the lead, I got into the shower and he followed suite. The entire time we were in the shower his dick was semi hard, but he didn't try anything. He washed my back, and I washed his.

"Mmmm, damn." Was I dreaming or was there really a tongue exploring my treasure? This was my first time ever having someone put their mouth on me, but this was definitely something that I could get used to. Opening my eyes, I looked down and there was Storm, hair tied up in a bun between my legs eating away like he was hungry, and I was the only thing that could curb his appetite.

He looked up and that's when our eyes met. I didn't know it was possible, but he looked even sexier with my pussy in his mouth. That look turned me on even more and before I knew it I was having a gut wrenching orgasm, the first I had ever experienced. It took everything out of me and I had this euphoric feeling as if I was on a cloud.

Coming from between my legs, he brought his face to mine and gave me a kiss. Our tongues did a dance of their own, and my pussy became even more moist than it already was. I wanted him inside of me in the worst way, and I was hoping he would oblige.

Breaking the kiss, I spoke just above a whisper," Put it in."

Storm looked at me like he was unsure if I had just spoken those three words, or maybe he was looking at my face to make sure that I was ready; and I was. There was no uncertainty on my end. He took my bottom lip into his mouth and then I braced myself for what was to come.

"Fuckkk," I moaned as he started to enter me. He went slow, but it still hurt. Eyes closed and trying to relax, he finally got it all the way in and it started to feel good, hell great even.

"Damn Skyy." There was an animalistic look on his face. Lifting up, he backed up and I wrapped my legs around his back. He was grinding in and out of me slowly, but with force.

The entire bed was rocking as he started to pick up the pace. I could feel myself on the verge of cumming.

"I'm about to cum again," I screamed.

"Fuck, me too. Cum on my dick." And just like that we came in unison. We were both out of breath, and sweaty even though the central air was on. Getting out of bed, we both went into the bathroom to wash off and then laid back down. My head was on his chest and before I knew it he was snoring, and I followed right behind.

Chapter 15

Chiasia

"Yo, grab that for me! It's probably the food!" Chinx yelled from the shower and I almost jumped out of my skin. We had just gotten done having a morning of sex, and we were both hungry. For some reason, Chinx didn't like taking showers together, so while he was in there I was in his phone trying to unlock it. So far, I had tried his birthday, 000, 1234 and other simple codes that men used; but I had no luck.

"Okay!" I yelled back and went to open the door, without checking the peep hole.

I expected to see a delivery person with the pizza we had just ordered from Dominos, but nope it was a woman standing there looking just as surprised to see me as I was at seeing her. She was an older woman; she was pretty though. She was wearing a black pencil skirt with a white blouse and she had a pair of black flats on her feet.

Oh damn, I thought. I had opened the door for a Jehovah's witness.

"Ummm, how can I help you?" I asked. Maybe she was lost, maybe she had knocked on the wrong door, but I was half expecting her to pull a flyer from somewhere and start to tell me all about her religion.

"Is Chinx here?"

"Wait a minute." Closing and locking the door, I walked into the bathroom where Chinx was just getting out of the shower. If it wasn't for the woman at the door I would be jumping his bone again.

"That was the food?"

"Nope it's some woman at the door looking for you."

"Man, stop playing. Nobody came to that door but some damn food." He opened the medicine cabinet, grabbing two Q-tips and started cleaning his ears.

"I'm serious. It's a light skinned woman at the door. She's pretty, but dressed like a Jehovah's witness but I don't know what you're into."

With a weird look on his face, he walked quickly to the door and looked through the peephole. He unlocked it quickly and swung it open. The look on his face was a weird one. It looked like he had seen a ghost and with the mouth that Chinx had on him; I had never seen him speechless.

"Hey, son." Now, I didn't know what to say and honestly, I didn't want to be the awkward person in the room, so I dismissed myself to the living room. About 10 minutes later Chinx was coming into the living room with the food we had ordered. Now I knew there wasn't something right with the visit from his mom. He didn't play about his all white living room, you couldn't eat or have shoes on in here.

"Are you okay?"

"Yea, why?" he asked sitting the food on the table and taking a seat on the couch.

"Because you brought food into your white living room." I pointed out.

Looking around, it was like he just noticed but he saved face by replying," I just wanted us to chill and eat in here."

"Okayyy." I wanted to ask him what that whole thing was about and where his mom had gone, but we hadn't been together that long. Also, there were some things people just had to want to talk to you about. You couldn't force them.

I pulled up to my house and pulled into the driveway behind my mother's car. Lately, my father had been letting me use his car more and I was grateful for that. Getting out of the car, I noticed Skyy's mother in front of the house. She kept looking at the house door, like she was waiting for someone.

"Hey! What are you doing here?" Skyy's mother jumped as if I had startled her. She was looking more nervous than ever.

"Oh, nothing. Just waiting."

"Waiting for what? Skyy isn't here." I knew they hadn't been talking but maybe she wanted to mend their relationship. "I can call or text her and see where she is if you wanted to talk to her. She's not answering your calls?"

Pulling my phone from my back pocket, I was ready to dial Skyy's number and let her know that her mother was looking for her and ready to talk.

"Oh no, no Chiasia honey, that's okay. I'm waiting for your father."

"Ohhh okay. See you later." I turned around and started back towards the house. The conversation was a little off, but nothing could prepare me for what I was about to walk into.

"So, you're fucking that bitch? You can get the fuck out!" This is what I walked into when I walked through our front door. My mother was yelling at my father and this was so unlike them. To me, they had this picture-perfect marriage, but now she was telling him to get out. "Do you think that I'm stupid? You think I can't see how you two flirt with each other? She's a hoe, she flirts with anybody, but you get that stupid ass goofy grin, eating out the palm of her fucking hand."

Going up the stairs slowly, I was shocked at the sight in front of me. There was my father standing outside of the bedroom door and his clothes were being thrown out of the room. They were hitting him in his face, the floor by his feet, behind him. There were basically clothes all through the hallway. He was standing there, looking defeated but not saying much of anything.

"What's going on?" My father looked over to me like he was embarrassed, and he probably was. They always made it a point to make sure not to argue in front of me. I mean, yea there were some times where I could sense the tension or where they weren't talking as much. But this was a different level.

"Your daddy taking his dirty ass dick and moving out. That's what's going on!"

"Charlene, don't talk like that in front of our daughter!" Since, I'd been here this was the first time I had heard my father respond to her.

"In case you haven't realized, our daughter is basically a grown ass woman. And she'll see you around town with the whore anyway. Now like I said, get the hell out of my house."

"Ummm, dad Skyy's mother is outside. She said she's waiting for you?" The confusion was hesitant all in my voice because for the life of me I couldn't figure out why she was waiting for him.

"You brought that bitch to my house?!" Before I could even wrap my head around what was just said, my mother was flying out of the room and was on my father like white on rice. My mother was a shorter woman while my dad stood about a foot taller than her. She was beating into his chest with tears coming down her eyes and he was letting her.

It was an emotional scene, and I honestly didn't want to be here for it. Especially because now I could see exactly what the issue was and whose fault it had been. Turning around, I ran back down the stairs and out of the house.

Getting into my dad's car I pulled out of the driveway and pulled up to Skyy's mom in her car.

"You home wrecking whore!" I yelled as I pulled off into the direction of Skyy's house. I needed answers and I needed them now.

"Why didn't you tell me?" There were tears coming down my face when she opened the door. The entire ride there I had been in hysterics. How could a perfect night and morning with Chinx turn into something so terrible? How could a 20-year marriage be over just like that?

"What? What happened? Are you okay?" Skyy asked. She opened the door and closed it behind me as I walked into her house.

Standing in the middle of the room where the couch was, I asked the question again," Why didn't you tell me?" She looked at me confused. Maybe she didn't know, I told myself. But it was something that told me she did.

"Chi, I have no idea what you're talking about right now? What's going on?"

"My father and your mother. Why didn't you tell me?" That's when I saw it. There was guilt and embarrassment written all over her face.

"Chi, I swear I wanted to, but I didn't know how. That's why we got into it and why I moved out. I see how your parents are. They were like the model family ya know? Then to see your father messing with my mom." She shook her head before continuing," I knew it was shady as hell and I just didn't know how to tell you."

"But I'm your best friend!" I yelled. My emotions were running high and it had me yelling at my best friend, my sister.

"And that's my mother. Even if I don't agree with what she does, that's my mom."

"Your mom's a whore Skyy! Now my mother and father are breaking up because of that home wrecker."

Putting her hand up she spoke," Whoa, wait. I understand that you're mad Chi, trust me I understand but the name calling, don't do it. That's still my mother no matter if she's right or wrong."

"You're defending her. She basically kicked you out because she was sleeping with a married man. Not a random married man, my father!"

"Your father that's a grown man! He made a choice too, my mother wasn't the only one in the wrong. I love you Chi and I'm sorry. Truly, I am, but both our parents are grown; they made a choice, and I hope that their choice doesn't mess up our relationship." I didn't know what else to say; she was right.

Walking up to my friend for years, I broke down. In her arms, in the middle of her studio; I cried until there was nothing left.

Chapter 16

Storm

I came up from nothing nigga you can't tell me shit yeah

Did it on my own, check out neck check my wrist yeah

I swear I ain't never expected it to be like this

Now a nigga gettin' rich I swear everyday we lit yeah

Everyday we lit yeah, you can't tell me shit yeah

'Member I was broke yeah, now I'm gettin' rich yeah

Yeah when yo' diamonds colder than a bitch, then you know

you lit

When you quick to take a nigga bitch, then you know you lit

Everyday we lit yeah everyday we lit yeah

Everyday we lit yeah everyday we lit yeah

Everyday we lit everyday we lit

Everyday we lit yeah, everyday we lit

Chinx and I were on our way to check out my spots and make sure shit was straight. We did this a couple days out of the week. We had 5 spots set up through the city and we saw them on random days. Never the same and there were 2 reasons for that. I didn't want anybody to be able to pinpoint my movements, and I didn't want my workers getting comfortable.

They knew I could pop up at any given time and they needed to be on their P's and Q's. The first spot we went to was the one in the jets. We got out and headed into the building.

"Yo, my mom been stopping by my house," Chinx said out of the blue. He had been quiet, but that was normal. Chinx wasn't a big talker same as me, so there was never really a lot of talking when we were together. But he was like my brother and I felt that his vibe was off, and now I knew why.

"Word?" We were walking up the stairs of the building.

"Hell, yea man. She said she got herself cleaned up and wants to build a relationship with me."

Nodding my head, I responded," Cool, what you gonna do?"

"Shit, I don't know." We reached the door to the spot and knocked. At the same time, as before Candy opened her door as if we were coming to see her.

"Hey Storm, hey Chinx," she spoke to us both. "Storm would you be able to help me. My blinds in my room fell down and I can't get it back up."

"I don't really have time ma."

"Please, it'll just be a second I swear." Candy was looking at me with a pleading look on her face.

"Iight man." The door to our spot opened and Chinx walked in while I went across the hall to Candy's. With all the kids she had, I was surprised that her home was almost spotless. There were a couple of toys here and there but besides that, it was clean.

"Follow me, my room is right over here." The set up was the same as the apartment across the hallway so I was familiar with it. Walking behind her, I couldn't help but look at her ass; it was nice, big and round. She was wearing a pair of red and white striped shorts and a white crop top that showed off her slim waist.

We walked into her room and she had it set up nicely even though she had an old school bedroom set. It was the one where the bed had the mirror on the headboard and all I could think was how many years she'd had it and how many niggas she'd fucked on it. Candy had all those kids, so if she fucked them raw, I'm sure they weren't the only ones. The other niggas just didn't get her ass pregnant.

"Here it is." She handed me the blinds that were laid on the floor and gestured towards the empty window. Taking it from her hand, I put the blinds up easily and in less than 2 minutes.

"Iight, imma be out of here now." I turned to walk out of the room door, which was on the other side of the bed, but Candy jumped in front of me.

"Why are you rushing off so quick? Would you like something to drink?"

"No, I'm good. I really have to go yo."

"Well, let me thank you, please." She closed her room door and dropped down to her knees right in front of me. Before I could object, she was unbuckling my pants and trying to get them down.

"Nah, you good. It was just a blind." I tried to push her away, but not really with too much force.

"Let me just taste you." Finally getting my jeans and boxers down, she wasted no time putting her warm mouth on my dick. She took it all in, without gagging. Putting both of my hands up, I held onto the wall, bracing myself.

"Damn," slipped out of the mouth quietly.

"Mmmm, let me see how you taste." Candy took both of my balls into her mouth and sucked on them as she jacked my dick at the same time. The shit was feeling so good and I could feel my balls tighten; I was ready to cum. Without me having to say anything, Candy put my dick back into her mouth and let my cum go down her throat.

I opened the door to the apartment and all eyes were on me.

"What the fuck is up?" I asked the room full of eyes staring at me. They all started dying laughing.

"You fucked that hoe, didn't you?" Biggs asked. He was a heavyset nigga that had been down with the team for a minute. He was a funny nigga too and always had jokes.

"Hell nah, I ain't fuck her. But you did though didn't you?" I said back, and everybody laughed. Everybody knew Biggs loved all the project hoes. Most of them he had fucked with, shit I was surprised he didn't have babies running all around the jets.

"You know I did. Her pussy aight, but she sure could suck a dick though!" Now we were all laughing, but I never mentioned that I agreed. She sure could suck a dick though!

"Skyy!" I had just gotten home and was taking my shoes off. Skyy was supposed to be staying the night, and I had just gotten home from a long day. My truck was in the garage, so I knew she had to be here. There was something that I wanted to show her.

Going upstairs I went into my room and she was on the bed knocked out. There were school books sprawled all over the bed and it looked like she had fallen asleep while studying.

"Skyy, baby wake up." I shook her awake. It took a minute, but finally her eyes opened. She had a sexy sleepy look and if I wasn't trying to show her something and didn't still have Candy's saliva on my dick; she would have been bent over before she could get her marbles together.

"I gotta show you something, come on get up." Skyy stretched and went to get out of bed when I noticed she was naked. "I thought you were studying, why the hell you naked?"

"I like to study naked. What do you need me to see?" Her chocolate, sun kissed nipples were staring back at me as she spoke. The air had her nipples standing at attention. I had to get my mind back right because I refused to indulge before I took a shower.

"It's outside. Throw something on."

"Okay!" she yelled excitedly.

Covering her hands with my eyes, we walked outside to the front. I was guiding her down the front steps and then over to the surprise I had waiting for her. Taking my hands from her eyes, I let her see just what I had for her.

"Oh my god, oh my god. Is this mine?"

"Yes."

"Ahhhhh," she screamed as she hugged me and kissed me all over my face. There was a candy red 5 series BMW coupe with a white bow on it. The inside was custom, all-white and her name was embedded on the driver's side chair and my name was embedded in the passenger seat. Skyy sat in the driver's seat, so I sat in the passenger.

"You like?"

"Like? I love it! Thank you so much! Why did you get it for me? I know I've been using your truck, I was working on getting my own." She was talking a mile a minute.

"Chill, chill, chill. I got it for you because I wanted to. You needed a car, and this is the one I want you to have. This is not all though."

"There's more? No, I can notttttt," she said imitating Joseline from Love an Hip Hop and I had to laugh. She had me watching that shit lately, so I actually understood the joke.

"You a damn fool. Check the visor." My phone vibrated as the words left my mouth and it was a text from Yas asking what I was doing. Silencing my phone, I put it on my lap and waited for Skyy to open the envelope I had waiting for her. She opened the envelope and again my face was showered with her soft lips.

"What did I do to deserve you?" she asked with a smile on her face.

"No, what did I do to deserve you Skyy?"

Chapter 17

Chinx

It was early morning, and I was sitting at Ihop waiting for my mother. Usually I wouldn't be the first one to meet with anybody, but this meeting had me kind of anxious. She had been stopping by the apartment trying to get me to reconcile with her and I was considering it, but every time I saw her the memories flooded back.

Nobody knew the extent of the shit I went through before I stayed with Storm and his mom. Shit was rough, and my mother seemed to not give a fuck about nothing. They say the worst pain was heart break and I know my father left but what about me? She just gave up on me and our household like my father was the only thing that mattered.

After 10 minutes of sitting and waiting, finally the woman of the hour walked through the door. She noticed me almost immediately because the place wasn't packed at all and walked over to where I was sitting. She sat down and looked at me with a smile on her face.

After all of these years, my mother was still beautiful. Even though the drugs made her lose some weight it hadn't diminished her beauty a bit. My mother's face was clear of blemishes and wrinkles.

"Hey, son," my mother said.

"What's up? I ordered us some water," I pointed to the 2 glasses on the table.

"Thank you."

"So, what's going on? What did you want to talk about?"

"Chinx, I know I've made some mistakes and there are things I can never come back from, but I really want us to have the bond that we used to. Yes, I know there's a lot I've missed but if you would let me back in I would really appreciate it."

"And the drugs?" If the drugs weren't a for sure thing of the past, then there was no way that we could mend anything. When she was on drugs she was a different person that would do anything just to get high.

"I'm in NA. I've been going to meetings 3 times a week and I have been clean for 365 days now exactly. Today makes a year of my sobriety."

"What made you stop?" It was a question that was in the back of my mind. Losing me didn't even make her stop, so what was the last straw for her exactly.

"I met a man. We both were battling our drug addictions, and we decided to get clean together. We are actually getting married soon and I want you to walk me down the aisle."

Chuckling, I didn't know whether I should yell or laugh. I knew there was a reason she was trying to reconcile with me all of a sudden and it had nothing to do with building a better relationship with me. She just wanted somebody there to walk her down the aisle and probably pay for some shit.

"I thought the first step in being sober was to not have a significant other?" The look on my face let her know that I was hip to her bullshit. That's all this was anyway. Bullshit.

"Well, it is. But.." she started.

"But what?" I was waiting for a logical explanation, but something was telling me that she didn't have one. "Yo, I only did this lil meeting shit because I felt bad for you and I thought that maybe just maybe you cared about me instead of a nigga or just yourself. I see it's the same damn thing from before."

Getting up from the table, I threw some money on the table told her to enjoy breakfast on me and was out the door.

Chapter 18

Skyy

I was smiling ear to ear as we touched down in Miami. Storm had surprised me with a car and a first-class trip to Miami. This was my first time ever being to the South and I was beyond ecstatic. Of course, Chi and Chinx were with us and I couldn't wait to see what the city had in store for us.

After getting our bags, we were greeted at the door by 2 men with 2 very nice cars. Storm had it set up for the exclusive rental company to bring the cars to us, so we didn't have to worry about catching an Uber or Lyft to pick up the car. The cars that we had were an Audi and a Benz. They were both black interior and exterior.

We got into the Audi while Chi and Chinx got into the Benz. I was so in love with the Audi as soon as my ass touched the seat. The new car smell, and the leather was soft as butter. They followed behind us as we went to the hotel. There wasn't much conversation as I took in the sights and Storm was following the GPS and blasting his music.

The scenery was amazing from the buildings, to the trees and even the people. To say the least, I was in awe. After about 20 minutes of driving we pulled up to the hotel we were staying at, Fontainebleau. I had heard of this hotel on Instagram when Fabolous stayed there, so this now had me even more excited and ready to see what the hype was about.

We pulled up to the front and valet was ready to take the car, but before we got out I had something that I wanted to say.

"Storm, thank you again for this trip." I was thanking him for the umpteenth time and although he said it wasn't needed it was the least I could do. He was about to speak when I held up my hand to stop him. "I know, I know, I don't have to say thank you, but I want to."

"As long as you know. Ya man will do anything for you." I was all smiles as the valet came to each side, opened our doors and we stepped out.

After checking in, both couples departed as we headed to our rooms. We were on the same floor but on opposite sides. We walked in the suite and I was in love. It was decorated in neutral colors, white, cream with a touch of grey. It was set up into 3 rooms. There was the living room, bathroom and bedroom; all 3 were spacious.

Opening the patio door, I stepped out and we had a full view of the beach. There were people jet skiing, tanning and playing volleyball.

"You like it?" Storm came up behind me and wrapped his arms around me.

"I love it." There was a big smile on my face that only he knew how to bring out of me. Turning around to face him, I kissed him until we were both out of breath but left wanting more.

At this moment, I was so happy that I took him back, but he better not fuck up again. He didn't know it, but if he so much as text messaged another chick I was out of this relationship. Storm was my heart, but I wasn't about to keep letting him treat me like shit when I knew that I deserved more.

"Mmm, come show daddy how much you love it." Storm said as he sat in the patio chair. That was all that needed to be said.

Pulling his pants and boxers down right there on the patio, I pulled my leggings down and started to ride him from the back. Bouncing up and down on his dick, Storm's hands were on each of my thighs guiding me. My eyes were closed, and my head was tossed back as his dick plunged in and out of me.

"Shit baby," I moaned as I felt myself about to have an orgasm.

"Go ahead baby, cum on my dick." His words made my pussy wetter and before I couldn't even worry about him getting off, I was coating him with my juices.

"I'm coming now baby," Storm yelled out as I massaged his balls with my hand, feeling them tighten as he released inside of me.

Clap, clap, clap

Once we stopped there was clapping coming from the patio next to us. We looked over and there was an older couple, probably in their mid-30's clapping and congratulating us. Grabbing my pants from the floor, I slid the patio door open and rushed inside, embarrassment covering my face while Storm laughed.

"That is not funny. Oh my god, I'm so embarrassed."

"Why? You with ya man and they don't know you," he laughed again.

"Okay and what if they recorded us or something." I was freaking out, all I could think about was seeing Storm and I on MTO or World Star fucking on a hotel balcony.

"Girl, nobody recorded us. They just watched our little show. They're probably over there fucking each other right now; we just saved a marriage." He was joking but I was still mortified.

"Skyy, close the curtains and come ride this dick so we can take a nap." Putting my exposing thoughts to the side, I did just that.

3 hours later and we had fucked, showered and took a nap. Now we were getting dressed to head out for dinner and clubbing. I was putting my finishing touches on my makeup when Storm came into the bathroom. He had been ready for 20 minutes now and was just waiting for me.

"Yo, you almost ready. Chinx and ya girl waiting for us in the lobby."

"Chi? On time? That's a first, but yea I'm done." Smacking my lips, I put my lip gloss in my makeup bag and switched off the light to the bathroom.

On our way, down to the lobby Storm's phone rang while we were on the elevator. The first time he ignored it, but another call came back to back. Looking at my face he knew if he didn't answer it I would be asking who it was that he was avoiding.

"Hello," he answered on the second ring. He was silent for a moment just listening and then he spoke. "Thanks ma, but you a little early." He said looking at the Rolex on his wrist. "My birthday not for another 3 hours."

They talked some more until we reached the lobby, and he let her know that he was about to start driving, so he would call her back tomorrow. As soon as the call was disconnected I started to question him.

"Why didn't you tell me your birthday was tomorrow?" He hadn't mentioned that his birthday was coming up. I had made a big deal out of mine, but here he was acting so nonchalant about his.

"It's not important, that's why," he shrugged. Chi and Chinx stood up as we approached them, and I had to say my girl was looking niceeee. We had gone shopping before the trip and this outfit was one she couldn't see on herself, but I told her to go for it. She was wearing an off-white satin romper with a pair of red Giuseppe heels and had a red clutch as well.

Chi wasn't too sure if she could pull off satin, but I assured her she could, and she was pulling it off well. As we stepped outside, both of our cars were already at the front waiting for us with Hispanic men holding open each passenger door. Even though I didn't know it was Storm's birthday I was now excited and ready to bring it in with him.

Chapter 19

Storm

Hold up, hold up, hold up (What)

Let me catch my breath (Yeah)

Let me count these checks (What)

Flex on my Ex (Yeah)

They don't got no respect (I don't, I don't)

Break up in a text (What?)

Pull up in a G (Yeah)

T3 fly off in a jet (vroom!)

Pull up, I'm suited

And you know I got my toolie

Okay, I might Billy Coop it

Heard you pull up, mini cooper

Told that lil bitch that she stupid

Okay these niggas can't move me

Okay these bitches can't move me

Those are not diamonds, they're rubies

Wait that's not rubies, that's glass

Smack that bitch right on the ass (what?)

We had VIP turned the fuck up! The liquor was flowing, weed was being passed and the club was jumping. It was 1 in the morning, so it was officially my birthday. Skyy was to the left of me turned up, dancing with Chi. They were just as turnt as me like it was their birthday.

Looking over at Skyy, she was looking good as hell today. She had on a pair of yellow satin shorts with the matching spaghetti strap crop top on with it. My baby didn't like to wear heels, so she was wearing a pair of yellow Rihanna Fenty Puma sneakers. The yellow was complimenting the fuck out of her chocolate skin and I was feeling her like crazy tonight. Yea, once we got back to the hotel shit was going to get real.

While I was staring at her, her eyes met mine and she smiled at me with a seductive look. Nodding my head, I acknowledged her and that was all that she needed. Skyy knew what it was and from the look on my face she knew what was ahead of her tonight.

"Yo, my nigga you are getting old!" Chinx yelled over the music.

"Hell nah nigga, a nigga just getting better with time," I responded as I took a drink from the bottle of Moet that I was drinking from.

"Yo, so that shit I talked to you about the other day."
He was talking about his mom. Nodding my head, I
confirmed I knew what he was referring to.

"I don't think I'm going to give her ass a chance. We
met up and shit just wasn't right. Mom said I should give her
another try but I don't know."

"I respect it man, but even though she fucked up
that's always going to be your mother and if she's doing well
you should give her a chance."

"Yea. Any who enough of this sappy shit. Let's turn
the fuck up!" He took a shot to the head and handed me one
to do.

"You a funny nigga. I'll be right back, I gotta use the
bathroom real quick."

Walking to the back of the club I walked straight into
the bathroom. The club was jam packed, so I was surprised
there wasn't a line for the bathroom. There were 3 stalls and
there was a nigga in the first stall, so I went to the third.

Unzipping my pants, I threw my head back as I drained the main vein. I was so intoxicated that relieving myself was feeling so good.

Boom

As soon as I went to zip my pants back up, the door was being kicked in and 3 niggas rushed inside the bathroom. They all had dreads and gold in their mouth.

"Run them pockets nigga!" the one with the gun yelled. He was the only light skinned one while the other two were brown skinned.

"You know who you fucking with?" My voice was calm, there was not a hint of intoxication or bitch in my shit. I always said if I died it was going to be on both feet never knees in the dirt. My gun was tucked in my back, but I knew if I moved a muscle these trigger-happy niggas would waste no time filling me up full of lead.

"We don't give a fuck who you think you are. We do know ya pussy ass ain't from round here!" One of the other dudes yelled.

"Mane, fuck all that talking. Take everything off. I'll take those rings, earrings, shit that muthafucking watch shining like a muthafucka."

My mind was going at a mile a minute. I didn't know if I should take these niggas on or just give this shit up. It wasn't like I couldn't replace it, but that wasn't the point. These down south niggas were testing my gangster like I wouldn't hesitate to blow a nigga head off. Just as I was about to go for my gun, there was a gunshot.

Pop

The lock on the door was blown off and the door swung open. The three dread heads turned to look at the commotion and that gave me my chance. I pulled my gun from my back and took the safety off. Chinx walked into the bathroom with his gun pointed and ready to rock any nigga to sleep.

That was my nigga!

When the dreads turned back around to me, they knew they had fucked up. Their eyes immediately went to the pistol that was in my hand.

"Ah ah ah," I tormented them with a smirk on my face. "Funny how the tables turn huh?"

Chinx and I looked at each other. He hadn't spoken a word yet and I already knew what was on his mind, the same thing I had on mine; murder. With a grimacing look on our faces we started to put holes in these niggas. The light skinned tough ass one though, I shot his ass right in the head.

After lighting the bathroom, the fuck up, we knew we had to cut the night short and get the fuck outta there. Walking out of the bathroom, we kept our heads low and blended into the crowd. I made sure I looked at the entrance to the bathroom but there were no cameras. It didn't look like the club had cameras at all.

"Yo, let's head out the back door," Chinx said above the music just enough, so I could hear.

"Iight, after we get the girls."

"They outside waiting for us at the corner." Once we got out he let me know he knew something was wrong because I was in the bathroom for way too fucking long and he knew I wasn't shitting because I hate public bathrooms. Like he said, Skyy and Chi were both waiting behind the wheels of each car at the corner. We got in and peeled off back to the hotel.

"Babe, babe, look. Isn't that the club we were at last night?" Skyy was shaking me out of my sleep. Rubbing my eyes, I looked at the TV and in fact it was. They were talking about 3 armed men being killed in the club bathroom. Police were saying it looked like a love triangle gone wrong.

"Damn, that's crazy." Skyy was shaking her head as she looked at the screen like she was just appalled at the crime. Getting out of bed, I went into the bathroom to pee. While I was peeing, I had to laugh a little bit. Chinx and I had set it up, so it looked like a crime of passion.

It was Chinx's idea, and it looked like the extra 2 minutes had paid off. Those niggas had it coming to them trying to rob me in the bathroom like I was a sucka. If it wasn't for Chinx, I wouldn't have made it out of that bathroom because the way my pride set up I was ready to go to war. That's why it was always great to have a soldier on your side.

Buzz, Buzz

My phone rang on the nightstand as I walked out of the bathroom. Skyy had turned from the news channel, and was now watching that annoying ass dress show Say Yes to the Dress. Shaking my head, I grabbed my phone, and it was yet another missed call from Yas, but this time she left a message. It was a message of her yelling and saying that she was being rushed to the hospital and wanted me to come there. My heart started to thump and pick up speed.

I was panicking over a child that I didn't even know if it was mine, but what if it was? Thinking of a quick plan, I sent Chinx a message saying we had to go to NYC for some business asap. Now I had to think of something good to tell Skyy. Of course, I didn't want to end our trip but if something was wrong with my baby and I wasn't there I would feel bad in the long run.

"Yo, Skyy," I turned towards her.

"What's up babe?" she answered but her eyes were still glued to the TV. "Ewww she wants to spend 10,000 on that ugly ass dress. Umph. What's up babe?" Now her eyes met mine. "What's wrong?"

"I gotta handle some business in NYC, so we have to cut this trip short. I'm sorry and I promise to bring you back soon as I can. But I mean u like New York, right?" The least I could do was finish our trip somewhere else.

"Aww really Storm. We were supposed to do jet skis today. It's not something that can wait?" Her bottom lip was poked out and she was laying the guilt on me thick, but I couldn't just say fuck it to a baby that could be mine.

"I'm sorry baby, it's an emergency so we have to go, iight? Pack up our stuff and imma go down to the front desk and see about checking out early and getting a flight back home."

"Okay, but Storm?"

"Yea?"

"You owe me." She gave me a look, and I knew I would be paying for cutting this trip.

4 hours later and we touched down in NYC. Both of the girls had an attitude because the trip was cut short. Chi had been side eyeing me the whole flight like I was her nigga. Skyy was mad but her shit was subtle, she was just extra quiet and when I asked her what was wrong she just said her stomach hurt.

I turned my phone back on and there were 5 text messages and 2 voicemails from Yas. She was asking where I was and how long it was going to take me to get there? I didn't even listen to the messages, but I sent her text letting her know I was on my way. We got the girls a cab to the hotel and we got in our own. I let Skyy know it might be a while but made sure to give her money in case they wanted to do anything. Also, I made sure to let her know that room service was of course on me so order whatever they wanted.

"Babe, make sure you text me when you can, so I know you're okay. Okay?" Skyy looked at me and said with her beautiful brown eyes and thick full lips. She was beautiful, and I wished it was her that was pregnant instead.

"Iight, imma hit you." I gave her a kiss and closed the cab door, and they sped off. Chinx and I got in ours we were on our way as well.

"Metropolitan hospital." The cab driver sped off and we were on our way.

Chapter 20

Skyy

I was so disappointed that Storm had to cut our trip short, but I mean business is business. The girlfriend I didn't want to be was the one that stopped my man from making money, even though it wasn't a legit job.

"He better not put us up in no cheap ass hotel." We were on our way to the hotel in the cab. I may have been mad, but Chi was madder.

"Girl, shut up," I laughed. "Storm would never put us in no cheap shit. Why didn't you tell Chinx you wanted to stay since you're so mad?"

We were both disappointed, but I didn't want to keep hearing about it. The whole flight she was looking at Storm like he had spit in her breakfast that morning.

"And I saw how you were side eyeing my man heffa."

"You did?" Chi laughed. "My bad, you know I can't hide my face when I'm mad."

"Yea, I know." We pulled up to the hotel and Storm was already making up for the Miami trip. The hotel he had us staying at was the Four Seasons and it was beautiful.

After checking in, Chi and I both went into our own rooms. When I got to the room, on the bed was edible arrangements and a bouquet of red and white roses. A smile was immediately plastered across my face. Opening my phone, I made sure to send Storm a text saying thank you and I love him.

It was my first time saying I love him and I was hoping he felt the same. Instead of waiting there with my phone in my hand for his text I went over to the window to check out the view. It was great. There were so many buildings each one higher than the next.

Buzz, buzz

My phone vibrated, and I dived onto the bed to retrieve it. It was Storm saying anything for his lady and he loved me too. I was blushing, harder than I had ever blushed before and my pussy was throbbing anticipating when he was back. I sent him a string of emojis the eggplant, a kissy face and the water squirting. He knew what it was.

Knock, knock, knock

"I don't want anyyyyy," I yelled through the door because I knew it had to be Chi.

"What are you doing in here?" she walked in as soon as I opened the door. "Dang, now I gotta curse Chinx out because I didn't get any edible arrangements or flowers." She sat on the bed and started to open the edible arrangements.

"Damn, I didn't even eat any yet. Don't eat my strawberries!"

"Skyy, nobody gonna eat ya damn strawberries. I know how much you like them. I'm hungry, you're not hungry?"

"A little bit, but my stomach is feeling funny." It had been feeling funny since this morning. I had a bit of a nauseous feeling, but then it was cramping a little too. My period wasn't supposed to be coming on for another 3 weeks or so.

"See, you hungry." Chi got up and grabbed the menu from the nightstand and started to finger through it. "Oooo this looks good." She pointed to a picture of shrimp and scallop with angel hair pasta.

"Even though I'm not hungry it does. Order me some too."

"Arrghhh," I was woken out of my sleep with excruciating pain. My stomach had been feeling funny with cramps here and there all day and night but now the pain was becoming unbearable. Storm still wasn't at the hotel yet, but he had sent me a message and told me that he would be here as soon as possible but there was a lot going on. I grabbed my phone from next to me on the bed.

Chi was just going to have to go to the hospital with me; something wasn't right. I sent her a text message, and she responded almost immediately. She was a night owl, so I knew she would be up. She told me to throw some clothes on and meet her downstairs, she was going to tell the front desk that we needed a cab.

15 minutes later we were headed out of the hotel and into the cab. My stomach still had not let up. I decided not to send Storm a text right now because I didn't want him to worry until I knew what was going on. Maybe I was just having the worst menstrual cramps ever.

"Metropolitan," I let the driver know as soon as we got into the cab.

While waiting to be called to the back by the nurse, I went through my phone. There were messages and calls from Lou that I hadn't picked up, returned or replied to. He had been trying to get in touch with me for days, but I didn't know how to tell him that I had decided to be with Storm. He was such a nice guy, and I knew that he was into me, so it was going to be hard to tell him.

Looking over his messages they were basically all the same. Lou had been saying good morning, what's up, and everything else to spark a conversation. The last message however was different, and something about it was right. He was saying that he was going through some shit and he really needed somebody to talk to. He had sent that text message a couple of hours ago.

I had time and since Storm wasn't around, I decided to write back and see what was up. Even though I didn't want to be in a relationship with him, I still wanted to be friends and being there for him was a part of being a friend. 5 minutes later he sent me a lengthy message about what was going on. Reading the message, I immediately recognized the situation and was wondering if it was the same one.

Apparently, his cousin from out of town that he was close to was murdered. Lou said he was found in a bathroom with his best friend and another dude that he chilled with. He said the news was saying some bullshit about it and he knew that wasn't the case. He was bugging out and needed to vent, he needed a friend to talk to.

I asked him where did his cousin live and what was the news saying. Of course, I already had an idea that it was the same thing I saw on the news. We ended up leaving the club early because Chinx said Storm wasn't feeling good. He said he had gotten too drunk way too quick and was in the bathroom throwing up.

Come to think of it Storm wasn't really all that drunk when we left, and he wasn't acting sick. We actually ended up having sex a couple of times and then I fell asleep in his arms. He couldn't have or could he? Nah, I thought stopping the idea that was trying to invade my mind. Almost immediately, Lou texted back and just like I thought it was in Miami.

The police and the news were saying it was a love triangle gone wrong. Lou insisted that his cousin wasn't gay, and he knew that for a fact. I saw the men's faces on the news and I had to admit that they didn't look like they were into men, but in this day and age, who knows? My stomach started to turn thinking of the possibility that Storm had something to do with their deaths, but we were there for vacation, and he didn't know them so why would he even get into it with them?

Just as I was about to text Lou back saying sorry for his loss and to let me know if he needed anything my name was being called to the back. Chi wanted to stay in the waiting room, but I wanted her ass in the back with me, so she was forced to come. Once I got behind the doors, they had me pee in a cup and took my weight.

"Undress and put this gown on and the doctor will be right in," the nurse said then walked out of the room, closing the door.

10 minutes of waiting and the doctor finally came back to the room. She introduced herself and then got down to the point.

"Okay, so we tested your urine, and it looks like you are pregnant! Congratulations!"

"What?" I asked, confusion lacing my voice.

"Yep. You are pregnant. Let's do an ultrasound to check on the baby. It is normal to have cramping early in the pregnancy, but I would like to just check and make sure everything is okay." I couldn't even speak, so I just nodded my head and waited as she got the gel and ultrasound machine.

"Oh my god, I'm going to be an auntie," Chi squealed and put her hands over her face. I laughed at her even though I was still in shock.

"Okay, here we go." The doctor turned on the monitor and then started to move the warm gel around my stomach. As she kept searching she went from having a smile on her face to now having a concerned look on her face. The glasses that were sitting on the bridge of her nose, she adjusted with her hand and continued to move the gel around.

The monitor was on, but there was nothing coming from it. I had seen it in movies and usually around this time, she would be pointing out a little bean to me and telling me how many weeks I was, but that wasn't happening.

"Is something wrong?" I asked. She was making me nervous.

Pursing her lips together, she turned off the monitor and started to wipe the gel from my stomach.

"It looks like you were 7 weeks pregnant and.."

Interrupting her before she could finish, I asked," What do you mean were?"

"I'm sorry honey. The fetus has no heartbeat."

"What? How?"

"It's very common with early pregnancies. This is the reason that you were experiencing cramps and the light bleeding. This does not mean that you can't have children. Many women have healthy full-term babies right after a miscarriage, sometimes thing like this just happens and there's many reasons for it."

"Okay." I was taking it all in, but the little excitement that I felt was now gone.

"I'm so sorry honey. What I'm going to do is go and get a prescription for some meds to help the rest of the tissue pass. I'll be right back," and with that she walked out of the room.

Did she just refer to the baby I lost as tissues?

"Oh my god, are you okay?" Chi was out of her seat and at my side now. There were tears in her eyes and a pitiful look on her face. She felt bad for me.

"Yea, I'm okay. It's not like I knew." I brushed it off as if it was nothing, even though I knew later I would be crying about it. How was I supposed to tell Storm that I had lost our baby?

The doctor was back in 10 minutes with a prescription for meds. She said that any bodega should be able to fill it for me as long as I had insurance. Before leaving the room, she said her condolences again and walked out. I got off the table and put my clothes back on. Chiasia and I weren't doing much talking and that was rare for us, especially her.

We both had too many thoughts right now though. She was probably wondering what to say to me and how to make me feel better. I was wondering how to channel my emotions and what I should tell Storm. This was supposed to be a fun vacation, and everything was turning sour.

Chi and I left out of the room and was headed to the elevator when we bumped into somebody. A somebody that was supposed to be handling business and I don't know how he could have been doing that in a hospital. Storm was standing there looking just as surprised to see me as I was to see him, but he also looked like he was trying to concoct a story in his head about why he was here.

Before he even had time, I asked him the golden question," Why are you here?"

"I told you I was handling business. I had some business in the hospital," he spoke nonchalantly. "Why you here ma?"

"Ummm," I didn't know what to tell him or how, but I didn't have much time to think about it. Storm's name was being yelled down the hallway before I could respond.

There was a woman with a hospital gown on, like the one I had just taken off. She was wobbling down the hall asking Storm why he was leaving and what was more important than this? Looking around him, as she got closer I got a better view of her and it was none other than the woman from the store, movies and bar. Now, I would say this was a coincidence, but it couldn't be, and my heart was telling me that it wasn't.

She was coming from the same way that Storm had just came from. The woman was talking to him as if I wasn't standing right there. As if I didn't exist. That wasn't even the most fucked up part. Looking at her, even through her hospital gown I could see her stomach bulging from underneath it.

"Storm, you're here with her?" Chi asked. She must have noticed that I couldn't find my voice. It was stuck in my throat, struggling to come out and deal with the situation that was in front of me.

"Man, Chi take Skyy and ya'll head back to the hotel. I'll be there in a minute." Turning around he spoke to the pregnant woman," You take ya ass back in that room. The doctor said the baby fine so the fuck I need to be here for?"

"Whose baby is that?" Finally, I had found my voice and the question that was hanging in the air was now right in front of Storm's face. There was nowhere he could go between Chi, the pregnant chick, me and the elevator taking forever. There was nowhere to run.

Storm turned and looked at me with pleading eyes. His thick eyebrows he had had come together and he looked like he wanted to speak but he didn't know what to say. This man had never been speechless before.

"Storm, whose baby is this?"

"Girl, are you fucking stupid? It's his baby. I know you didn't think that this community dick ass nigga was faithful. Ha ha, yea imagine that. This nigga slangs dick all from the city to the Roc."

"Bitch I wasn't talking to you! He's slanging dick but you're wobbling out here to keep him from leaving you in a hospital, so you must like it." I wasn't going to say shit to her because she didn't owe me any loyalty, but he did.

"Take ya ass on man!" Storm yelled, and she wobbled her ass back the way she had come.

"That's your baby?" The evidence was sitting in front of my face, but I wanted to hear it from him. It wasn't real until I heard the words come out of his mouth, from his lips.

"Skyy, I've been meaning to tell you," he started.

"Is it yours!" I yelled so loud that I knew we would soon have an audience, but I didn't care. There was no being around the bush about this. Either it was his baby, or it wasn't; there wasn't any in between.

"I don't know man," he put his head down in defeat.

"I hate you," I cried as I spoke. "I never knew that I could hate somebody, but I hate you. You're a lying trifling ass man. How could you sit in my face every day and act like you love me and care for me? How could you take my virginity and make me love you? You did all this knowing you had a baby or a possibility on the way! How fucking dare you Storm?!"

There were tears coming down my eyes and snot starting to come out my nose. I know I looked a hot ass mess, but I didn't care. This man had made a fool of me and broken me down to the last. This was the last straw.

Throwing the papers that the doctor had just given to me stating that I just had a miscarriage I yelled at him before getting on the elevator," Congratulations on your new baby and condolences on the one we just lost. Piece of shit." The elevator door closed just as he looked up at me and into my eyes. It was too late, I was done. Sometimes you could love someone, and the shit just wasn't meant to be.

Chapter 21

Yas

"Girl, where is Storm at? Did he really leave?" My best friend Key asked as soon as I walked back into the hospital room.

"He's in the hallway trying to kiss his "girlfriends" ass," I responded with quotation marks and all.

"His girlfriend? You never told me that nigga had a girlfriend," she responded looking at me like she was appalled.

"Storm just playing with that hoe. He'll be back fucking with me as soon as he's done with her." I sat on the hospital bed Indian style.

"So, you think that makes it any better? You need to stop playing a fool for him because you look stupid trying to be faithful to him while he's out here doing whatever to you."

"Key, don't." Putting my hand up, I signaled for her to just stop the lecture because it was really the last thing that I wanted to hear. She had a lot of nerve to talk about the nigga I was messing with when hers wasn't any better.

"I'm just saying. Anyway, let me go because Quincy's outside and I don't need him to start acting crazy.

See you later and text me when they discharge you." Key came to the bed, gave me a hug and was out the door. It was almost like he knew when she walked out because as soon as she did my phone was ringing.

"Hello."

"Hey, you good? How's the baby?" He was throwing questions left and right; I'm guessing because he didn't have that much time to talk.

"The baby's fine. I just had some bleeding and got scared, but they checked the baby on the ultrasound and he has a strong heartbeat and everything."

"He?"

"Oh yeah, we're having a boy," I said with a smile. He had expressed to me that he wanted a boy on many occasions.

"Damn, we got to start getting shit set up for lil man." As soon as he said that I heard the door in the background open and close.

"Hey baby, who are you on the phone with?" the woman in his background asked and I smiled anticipating the lie he was about to come up with.

"It's my sister."

"Oh, tell her I said hi."

"Aye, Key said hi."

Laughing, I responded," Yea, hi."

"Yo, we're about to head home, so I'll call you back."

"Okay bruh," I joked and hung up the phone.

Quincy was funny as hell. Like I said, Key could say whatever she wanted about Storm, but her nigga was playing her, and it was with me. Yea, I may look dumb at times for fucking with him, but she looked dumb all the time. There were times like today when I would be texting Quincy with a smile on my face and she would think it was Storm.

Speaking of Storm, he still hadn't made it back to the room and the only thing I could think of is that he left with that bitch of his. She was becoming a thorn in my damn side. Yea, I knew he wasn't my nigga, but he wasn't hers either. Storm and I had been fucking around with each other for a minute, and if he was going to settle down with anybody it was going to be me.

Scrolling through my contacts, I went to Storm's number and gave him a call. Of course, he didn't answer, so I called back and sent a couple of text messages. Feeling my baby kick, I rubbed my stomach and laid back in the bed. Storm and Quincy both thought that they were the father to my unborn child. Honestly, I didn't know who the father was.

Storm had the money, and I wanted my child to have the best. Quincy had money too, he wasn't hurting out here in these streets, but it was different money; different levels. Hopefully, I could get them both to take care of me and my child.

"Ugh," I grunted out loud. I was ready to get the hell out of this hospital. That whole bleeding thing was a damn lie. I was just social media stalking his bitch page and saw that they were on vacation. Vacation over, and hopefully their relationship was too since she now knew that I might be pregnant with his baby.

Getting out of the bed, I rushed to put my clothes on, so I could get the hell out of here. My plan was a success, but now I was ready to go home and see if Quincy could get away from Key. Storm would have to be put to the back burner for now, but I was going to get him. Even if it was the last thing I did.

To be continued...

CPSIA information can be obtained
at www.ICGtesting.com
Printed in the USA
LVHW010013200121
676949LV00043B/970